"Aren't you attracted to me?" Emma asked innocently.

Morgan didn't consider himself someone who got easily tongue-tied, but Emma's question caught him by surprise.

"My feelings don't matter," he finally croaked. "Acting on them would be inappropriate, under the circumstances."

His answer must have pleased her, because her full lips curved into a smile. In response, his own awareness ratcheted up a couple hundred notches. Just what he needed while they were alone in the wilderness.

"I'll take that as a yes," she drawled, giving him a wink.

While he was still trying to come up with a neutral comment to defuse the shimmering attraction between them, she slipped off her pack.

"Relax, Morgan," she said teasingly as she strutted away, hips swinging. "I'm not going to jump you."

PAMELA TOTH

USA TODAY bestselling author Pamela Toth is finally married to her high school sweetheart, three decades after graduation. They live in a town home with a cat and a view of Mt. Rainier.

She's always enjoyed doing jigsaw puzzles and she says that being involved in a series like LOGAN'S LEGACY is a lot like doing a puzzle with friends. One works on the sky, another the lake, a third the red barn. When they're all done, the sections fit seamlessly together—thanks to e-mail, skill and a lot of mutual support. She couldn't have found a better group to work with if she had handpicked them herself.

Pamela loves to hear from fans at P.O. Box 436, Woodinville WA 98072. For a personal reply, a stamped self-addressed envelope is appreciated.

LOGAN'S LEGACY

SECRETS & SEDUCTIONS
PAMELA TOTH

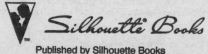

Published by Silhouette Books
America's Publisher of Contemporary Romance

Special thanks and acknowledgment are given to
Pamela Toth for her contribution
to the LOGAN'S LEGACY series.

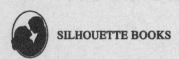 SILHOUETTE BOOKS

ISBN 0-373-61385-7

SECRETS & SEDUCTIONS

Visit Silhouette Books at www.eHarlequin.com

Printed in U.S.A.

Be a part of

Logan's Legacy

*Because birthright has its privileges
and family ties run deep.*

**The Children's Connection brought them
together...but would her quest for the truth
drive them apart?**

Morgan Davis: Morgan didn't trust himself
around women, but there was something different
about Emma. She was soft, loving, sexy—and the
attraction between them was unquestionable. But
did she care for him, or was she using him to find
the secrets of her past?

Emma Wright: Emma turned to the Children's
Connection for answers, but when handsome
Morgan Davis offered her a job, she found much
more. Morgan fulfilled her every desire, but she
knew he was hiding something—a secret that
could change her life forever....

But behind the scenes... Who was the mysterious
mastermind behind the trouble occurring at Portland
General?

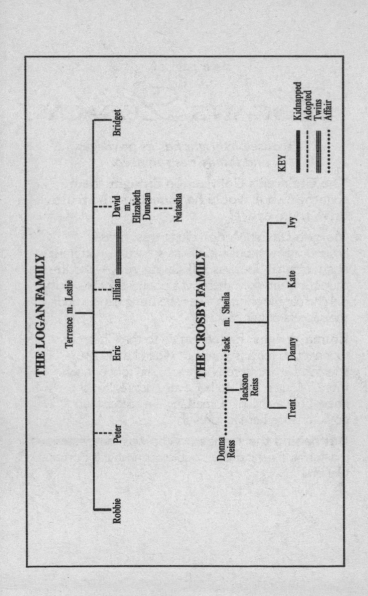

THE LOGAN FAMILY

Terrence m. Leslie

Robbie — Peter — Eric — Jillian — David — Bridget
m.
Elizabeth
Duncan

Natasha

THE CROSBY FAMILY

Donna
Reiss

Jack   m. Sheila

Jackson
Reiss

Trent — Danny — Kate — Ivy

KEY

Kidnapped
Adopted
Twins
Affair

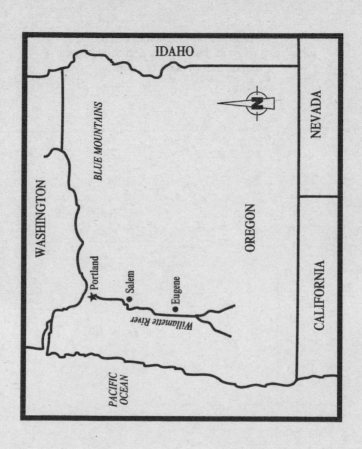

Dedicated to parents everywhere
who make room in their hearts and their homes
for children in need of both.

Prologue

Hands clenched tightly in her lap, school counselor Emma Wright tried to hide her apprehension behind a confident smile as she faced the Human Resources director. According to the local newspaper, a third of the maintenance staff and half the teachers' aides in the small Oregon school district where Emma worked had already been laid off because of budget cuts.

Emma's stomach had been in a knot ever since Sandra had asked her to come into the office. As the director flipped open the folder containing Emma's records, Emma hoped desperately that the reason for the summons had been to find out whether she could increase her workload, divide her time among more schools.

"I'm sure you're aware of the cuts we're facing for the new school year," Sandra said with a rueful expression as her gaze finally met Emma's.

Emma lifted her chin, forcing it not to wobble. "Of course." She gripped her hands together even more tightly, worried that the time she had missed after her miscarriage would be counted against her. "It's always a disappointment when education's not a priority, isn't it? I'm ready to do everything I can to help."

What she wanted desperately was to argue her case and to point out how badly the younger children in the district needed her. The other counselor, an older man, had an intimidating manner that seemed to scare them.

"I'm so glad you understand," Sandra said, her smile giving Emma a boost of reassurance. "Your evaluations have been excellent, so I'm sure you'll have no trouble finding something else."

For a moment Emma was stunned. "What are you telling me?" she asked through lips that suddenly felt like rubber. A rush of noise, like the sound of a jet engine, filled her head.

"Klaus has been here longer, so the district really has no choice." Sandra spread her hands wide. "I know you've experienced some personal trouble, but perhaps this will give you a chance to start fresh. I'm so sorry, but we won't be renewing your contract for the new school year."

Emma slumped back in her chair, feeling as though she'd been shot. "I see," she croaked.

Since her divorce, work had been her lifeline. She loved this job. Worse yet, with all the bills she'd been stuck with, her paycheck was a necessity.

Sandra slid back her chair, a signal that the interview was over. Her husband was an attorney in nearby Portland, so she probably didn't even need to work. "Be sure to let me know if there is anything I can do."

"Thank you." Emma's reply was automatic as she got to her feet on legs that trembled.

Sandra's bright smile was firmly in place when she circled the desk and opened the door. "Good luck."

Emma didn't have another "thank you" left in her, so she merely nodded before she walked back through the outer office. At least it was empty, so she didn't have to put on a happy face for the next clueless employee.

How much bad news was one person expected to handle without screaming, she wondered silently as she walked through the summer sunshine to her car? Two miscarriages, a divorce and now this.

When Don walked out, leaving her with a broken heart and a stack of bills, she'd been grateful for supportive parents and a job she enjoyed. In less than a week, she had lost both.

One

"Mr. Davis asked me to convey his apologies for running late. He'll see you just as soon as he finishes his call." The assistant adjusted her headset and smiled at Emma Wright, who was seated in the small waiting area.

The brass nameplate resting on the corner of the desk next to a potted plant with purple leaves read Cora Hanson. Behind her blond head, the tall windows framed a summer sky that was the same intense blue as the most precious turquoise jewelry.

"Is there anything I could get you?" Cora asked. "Coffee? Some water?"

Emma shook her head. "No, thank you. I'm fine."

Actually she had been anything but fine since first

learning about Children's Connection, an adoption agency associated with Portland General Hospital. Coffee would only make her more jittery. As for water, well, she didn't want any interruptions once she got in to see Morgan Davis, the agency director.

Scarcely able to contain her impatience after waiting a week for her appointment, Emma had arrived early at the sprawling medical complex. She was meeting a friend for lunch afterward and hoped to have some startling news to share.

After parking her car in the garage, she'd followed the signs directing her past lawns that were still green despite the dry July weather and well-tended flower beds exploding with color.

Now she flipped through the pages of a travel magazine without the slightest idea of what she saw there. Her hands shook with a combination of nerves and anticipation, her palms damp and her heart thudding.

She hadn't seen it coming, the bomb her parents dropped that shattered Emma's life as she'd known it. She hadn't suspected a thing, not until she looked into her mother's eyes and saw the lie. In just a few minutes, though, she would finally have what she needed to begin piecing the scattered bits of her life back together.

"Ms. Wright?" The assistant had sneaked up without Emma's notice to hover expectantly. "If you'd come with me, Mr. Davis will see you now."

Emma shot to her feet so fast that she actually felt

dizzy. Refusing to give in to the momentary weakness, she clutched her purse tightly as she followed the other woman down a short hallway. Ahead of her was an imposing set of double doors. One of them stood open.

Cora stepped aside and motioned for Emma to go on in.

A handsome black-haired man in a gray suit stood in front of a massive, heavily carved desk. The formality of his appearance made Emma feel slightly self-conscious about her own casual summer top and tan skirt.

"Ms. Wright? I'm Morgan Davis." He extended his hand, his grip warm and firm. "Won't you come in and have a seat?"

He nodded to his assistant, who shut the door quietly behind her. Emma took one of the purple tub chairs in front of the desk and the tall windows. Willing herself to be calm, she drew in a deep, slow breath.

Instead of returning to his black leather throne, the director surprised her by sitting in the chair next to hers. He was startlingly attractive, with deep blue eyes and cheekbones that would make a photographer weep. His dark tan was emphasized by his white shirt and maroon tie.

Ignoring the awareness dancing across her nerves, Emma stayed focused on her mission. She glanced over at the folder lying open on the desktop behind him. Did it contain the information she had come here to find?

He turned his head for a moment. His profile should have been on a stamp. His jaw was strong, his nose straight and his black eyelashes were as thick as the bristles of a paintbrush. Before she reeled herself back in, Emma wondered if the honey-gold tan of his face and hands extended to the rest of him.

"How can I help you?" he asked, lifting his brows. As he rested his hands on his thighs, a gold ring glinted on one finger.

Thank God he couldn't read her mind.

Emma crossed her legs, trying not to fidget, and moistened her suddenly dry lips. She'd planned so carefully what she wanted to say, but now her mind threatened to go blank.

"I just found out that your agency handled my adoption," she finally blurted out, lacing her fingers together tightly. "Is that my file on your desk?"

"That's right," he replied without turning his head. "As you can imagine, our records go back many years." He folded his arms loosely across his chest. His smile flashed even white teeth. "I hope there isn't a problem."

Sitting rigidly, she lifted her chin. The sense of injustice and pain still raged inside her. "The problem is that I wasn't told about it until a very short time ago."

He frowned, clearly puzzled. "About this agency?"

"About being adopted," she clarified. "I had no idea until now."

His expression softened as he leaned forward. "I'm so sorry." His voice was husky. "After all this time, the news must have come as quite a shock. I expect it's been difficult for you."

"Yes, very." She pressed her lips together to keep them from trembling. Her voice wobbled. "That's why I'm here, to find out what I can."

His frown returned. "I'll help in any way that I can, of course," he replied, "but I'm not sure what you're asking."

"I need the names of my biological parents," she said firmly. The Wrights had claimed not to have that information, but her faith in their honesty had taken a major hit and she wasn't sure that she believed them.

"If you don't mind my asking, how did this all come about?" He spread his hands wide. "After keeping your adoption a secret for all this time, what made them suddenly decide to tell you, do you know?"

His sympathetic smile and his show of interest threatened to shatter Emma's composure. Afraid she might break down and start sobbing, she clenched her teeth and stared down at her toes, painted red to match her shirt.

No one else except her parents—her *adoptive* parents, she reminded herself—knew the situation. Since she was no longer speaking to them, she'd had no one to confide in. She hadn't even told her close friend, Ivy Crosby, who'd been out of the country on business.

Ivy had been supportive throughout every bad thing that had happened to Emma, who was beginning to feel like a drama queen. Maybe she'd bring Ivy up to speed on her latest disaster over lunch.

Deliberately Emma stiffened her spine. "I found out just recently that I have a medical condition which is usually considered to be hereditary," she began.

His eyes narrowed with concern. "I hope it's nothing serious."

"Well, I'm not dying or anything like that," she said quickly.

He made a noncommittal murmur of relief.

There was no point in telling him about her endometriosis, a condition in which cells similar to those found in the uterus formed lesions in other areas of the body. It was a condition that sometimes caused a woman to miscarry.

"It's just that when I talked to my mother—" Emma shook her head and corrected herself "—my adoptive mother, it became obvious that I didn't inherit it from her."

Emma swallowed hard as she recalled her feeling of relief that Sally Wright hadn't had to suffer even the minor discomfort associated with the condition. Her reluctance to discuss it and her uncharacteristic nervousness hadn't raised Emma's suspicions until later, when she went back over everything she could remember about their conversation.

"I assumed then that I must have gotten the problem from the paternal side of the family," she continued, "but I was wrong."

"You discussed it with your adoptive father?" he asked.

"With my grandmother the next time I visited her. It

was obvious from what she said that she never experienced any of the symptoms."

Emma swallowed the bitter taste of regret. "Sometimes I wish that I had let the subject drop, but I can't go back, can I?" she asked the man seated across from her.

"If that were possible, I'm sure there are things in all our lives that we would change."

Was that sadness she heard in his deep voice, or merely empathy? With his looks and his position of authority here, plus whatever else he had going, did he still have regrets?

"What did you do after that?" he prompted her gently.

"I did some research on the Web," she admitted grimly, "and then I hotfooted it back to the Wrights' house with a couple of real burning questions."

"The Internet may not be the best place to get medical information," he reminded her. "There can be many different ways to interpret whatever you might find there."

"Oh, I know." Emma had been bluffing when she brought the subject up again. "I tried not to jump to any conclusions, but there was a look that passed between my parents—"

This time she didn't bother to correct herself as she bowed her head. The habit of more than a quarter of a century wasn't going to be changed in a matter of weeks, no matter the sense of betrayal burning in her heart.

"Anyway," she continued, blinking hard, "a red flag

went up and I just knew." She looked back at him. "At first they denied everything, but I kept pushing. Finally the whole sordid story came out."

Since he'd read Emma's file, he knew more about her right now than she did. "Are you sure that it's sordid?" he asked.

"That's what I'm here to find out."

His expression changed, becoming more wary. "What do you mean?" He touched the knot of his tie, as though it had suddenly gotten too tight. The flash of gold she had noticed on his hand earlier looked like a college ring.

Emma rolled her eyes. "After the big confession, they actually expected me to accept their apology, let the subject drop, to go on as though nothing was any different." She waved her hand in a gesture of dismissal. "But of course I can't do that."

It had been painfully clear to her that her adoptive parents had never intended to tell her the truth at all. Thank God the subject was no longer shrouded in secrecy.

"So that's why I've come to you." Emma gave him what she hoped to be a beguiling smile. "I'm here to find out about my real parents."

When he remained silent, a sudden feeling of panic gripped her and she couldn't resist glancing over at that open folder on his desk. What if it was incomplete? What if part of her file had been somehow lost, or destroyed in a fire or a flood?

"You do know who they are, don't you, the people who gave me up?" she demanded, her heart thudding in her chest.

"Whenever possible, we do like to have the records of both parents." The frown was back, causing a crease between his brows. If he kept it up, he'd be looking at Botox injections someday. "If you need another copy of your medical history, we'll be happy to provide one. My assistant can give you a form to fill out."

Suddenly breathless with anticipation, Emma pressed her palm to her heart. "I guess I didn't really take the time to make myself clear," she said. "It's not just the medical information that I'm after, it's everything."

His expression shifted, his frown lines deepening, and he seemed to lean away from her in his chair. "What exactly do you mean by *everything?*"

Emma balled her hands together in her lap. She wasn't going to give up now. "I need to know the names of my biological parents so I can find out if they're still alive." Her voice rose. "I might have siblings out there, family I never knew existed."

Contacting them would be a huge first step in taking back control of her life.

He had already started to shake his head before she finished speaking. "I'm sorry, but what you're asking is impossible. This agency can't help you."

Emma's mouth fell open as she stared at him, stunned into momentary silence.

"What do you mean?" she finally croaked as his refusal sank into her consciousness. "You just admitted that you have their names."

He spread his hands, palms up, in a helpless gesture. "That's true," he agreed, "but your file is confidential."

"Okay, I understand." Quickly Emma unzipped her purse. "I've got picture ID."

Before she could open her wallet, he surprised her again, this time by resting his hand lightly on hers. His touch was warm, but something about his gesture made her shiver as an icy chill slid down her spine.

"I'm so sorry," he said again as he let her go. "It's not just *your* confidentiality that our agency is sworn to protect."

His gaze held hers. "This was not an open adoption, so the only thing I'm allowed to share with you is your medical history."

Emma stared at him blankly. "But they're my parents. They'd *want* me to know who they are!"

Intellectually she knew that wasn't always true, but her emotions wouldn't let her believe it could apply to her. She wasn't going to be stonewalled! Panic shot through her. If she lunged across his desk and grabbed the folder, would she be able to read its contents before he got it away from her?

"Emma," he said quietly, startling her with his use of her first name, "I've read your entire file very carefully. There were no provisions made to give you contact information if you were ever to ask. Quite the contrary, there is a statement insisting on absolute privacy. I'm sorry."

She wasn't willing to give up, but she could tell by the set of his jaw that threats or pressure wouldn't change his mind. He appeared to be giving her time to absorb her disappointment.

"I see," she said, trying to sound reasonable.

"Are you all right?" he asked. "Would you like some water?"

"Yes, please." *Think,* she commanded herself while he went over to a sideboard and poured a glass for her. Frantically trying to come up with something to change his mind, she stared with fascination at the large blown-glass vase sitting proudly on a side table.

Talk about ugly!

When he came back and handed her the water, she took an obligatory sip before setting it down. "Thank you."

He was watching her closely, as though he expected her to do something crazy. Was there a secret alarm that he'd activated, calling for security? Somehow she doubted it. With his height and athletic build, he appeared more than capable of handling whatever she could dish out.

"Is there anything else I can do?" he asked when the silence began to lengthen between them.

Anything *else?*

"Surely there's another channel I can explore," she

said. "Some person I can talk to, an appeal process, *something,* in order to find out what I need?"

"I'm sorry. I'm afraid the buck stops with me."

Suddenly she had an idea. "You can contact them for me. They have a right to know that I'm looking for them, so they can give you permission to show me my file."

She was babbling, but she didn't care. "I'll swear on the Bible that I won't bother them if they don't want me to," she promised. "But society has changed a lot in the last twenty-seven years. Maybe they meant to revoke the 'no contact' order, but they forgot all about it. You could ask them."

"That's not possible." He looked genuinely regretful. "I'm sorry."

"Then what am I supposed to do?" she demanded, her frustration bubbling over.

"I know it sounds trite, but you have to accept the things you can't change," he said, spreading his hands wide. "I wish I could offer something more, but I can't."

"Accept?" Her voice rose like a hot-air balloon. "You want me to *accept* what I can't change?" She leaped to her feet, barely noticing that her purse had dropped to the floor, and leaned over Morgan Davis to look right into his killer blue eyes.

They widened slightly.

"Let me tell you what I've had to accept lately." She stuck her hand under his nose, fingers spread, and began ticking off items.

"I couldn't change my miscarriages or the divorce that followed." She tapped two fingers. "How about the layoff from my job as a school counselor? How was I supposed to change that?" There went another finger. "Unfortunately, none of the other districts around here are hiring, either, and I have bills to pay."

She hesitated, then decided that deserved a finger, too. "Maybe my creditors will have to accept not getting any money from me until I find another job, huh?"

He opened his mouth, but she cut him off ruthlessly. "If all that wasn't enough, I found out that I'm not even who I thought I was."

She waggled her splayed hand at him. "How can you tell me that not knowing my parents' names is just one more thing I have to accept?"

For just an instant he looked genuinely horrified before he quickly masked his expression. When he got to his feet, he was a head taller than Emma, who was forced to retreat.

"I wish there was something I could do," he said with apparently limitless patience.

"But you're the director," she cried. "I know you could make an exception if you really wanted to."

"No, I can't."

Stubborn ox! She had failed at so many things lately, being a wife, a mother, a successful counselor. How could she go away from here empty-handed?

Normally she hated whiners, but she was running out

of options. "No one else would have to find out," she wheedled softly. "I'd never let on where I got the information, I swear, please."

"Ms. Wright," he said.

Back to formality, she noticed.

"You may not believe me," he continued, "but I truly can understand your disappointment. However, this agency has entered into a contract with the people who entrusted you to us for placement in the first place. It's a binding legal document that I am not willing or able to violate."

Emma began to steam. Why had he told her the information was only a few feet away—to taunt her? How sadistic was that?

How could this petty bureaucrat in his fancy suit, sitting in his corner office like some potentate in his ivory tower, claim to know what she was feeling?

She had to try one last time, just in case he was beginning to weaken. "Are you sure there's nothing you can do?"

He shoved his hands into the pockets of his slacks and rocked back on the heels of what were no doubt very expensive shoes. "If you want to send me your résumé, I could ask around," he suggested with obvious reluctance. "Have you checked with the employment agencies here in Portland?"

"No!" Emma exclaimed, her frustration finally breaking through as she threw up her hands. "That's not the help I meant, and you know it!"

He shook his head. "Eventually you'll adjust to the idea that you were adopted by two people who wanted a baby very much," he insisted. "They should have told you a lot sooner, but they didn't. There it is and you can't change it."

If he said it was time to move on, she was going to slug him. Instead he shrugged.

"I've been doing this for a long while," he continued, apparently encouraged by her silence. "The adoption process isn't something that people go through unless they're desperate for a child. It's expensive and time-consuming. Their privacy is shredded, their lives picked apart."

He paused for breath while she gave him her iciest glare. "It sounds as though you've had a heck of a bumpy ride lately," he said, "but you look like a capable woman. Give yourself time to accept once again the identity that you've grown up with and the parents who raised you."

Emma's fuse, which had often been regrettably short, finally blew at the platitudes he was trying to heap on her poor head.

She picked up her purse. "You may think, just because you run this agency, that you're so wise and all-knowing about how it feels to be adopted, Mr. Davis." She grabbed the knob and yanked open the door, too angry to thank him for his time.

"As for your advice, your platitudes and your pseudo sympathy," she continued loudly, pointing at the big vase, "you can stick them right into that cheap, tacky glass monstrosity you seem to be so proud of."

Head held high, she sailed out the door and slammed it shut behind her.

Morgan stood in the suddenly silent office with his hands braced on his hips. He understood the reasons behind the agency's confidentiality regulations; he agreed with them one hundred percent.

In this case, Emma would never know that he was protecting her as well as her biological parents. She had been through enough without having to deal with a father who would never acknowledge her because the personal cost to him and his career might be more than he was willing to pay.

Between the shouting and door slamming, Emma Wright's exit had been a noisy one. At any moment he expected his assistant to burst into his office in order to reassure herself that he was still in one piece.

Absently he looked around, his glance landing on the large blown-glass vase that Emma had disparaged on her way out the door.

"It's not tacky," he muttered defensively as he studied the blue and purple sculpture. Created in the manner of Dale Chihuly, a prominent Northwest artist, the twisting, fluid shape resembled either a man-eating flower or a floppy hat, depending on the angle from which it was viewed.

"And it sure as hell wasn't cheap." Morgan winced as he recalled his winning bid at the recent charity auction. Even so, he would have willingly given up the vase in exchange for a magical elixir to remove that wounded, lost look from Emma Wright's sad gray eyes before she got angry and they turned to fire.

He had plenty of experience reading people, and the most satisfying part of his job was being able to help them. Emma's case was an unusual one, but she didn't know that and he couldn't tell her. It was part of the reason she stayed in his mind.

It had nothing to do with the fact that she was hot.

Portland was full of hot women wearing vividly colored cropped tops, tight miniskirts and miles of bare skin that replaced winter's long, dark raincoats and high boots. Quite a few of them worked right here in the hospital complex, but he'd gotten good at ignoring them.

His mother was always nagging him about giving her grandchildren, but he had rules about mixing business and pleasure. His rules hadn't protected him from Emma. Her red knit top hadn't been especially snug, nor did her short khaki skirt expose an unusual amount of her long, attractive legs. It was those big gray eyes that grabbed him first, eyes a man could dive into and get lost. Wavy brown hair he wanted to plunge his fingers into and muss all up.

Full lips...

His appreciation of Emma Wright as a woman wasn't

what she needed, so he forced himself to ignore the rush of heat as several rapid knocks sounded on his closed door.

"Enter," he called out as he turned away from the window.

Just as he had expected, it was Cora who poked her head inside. "Everything okay?" she asked.

As much as he was tempted to ask her opinion, he didn't have that luxury.

"Everything's fine," Morgan replied with a reassuring smile.

She studied him for another moment with a concerned expression, like a soccer mom checking for injuries, before she finally returned his smile with one of her own.

"Okay, good," she said. "Since you don't have any wounds in need of binding up, I'm going to lunch."

Around the corner from the assistant's station, Everett Baker had pressed himself against the wall so that he wouldn't be discovered. He'd been on his way back to the accounting department where he worked when he heard the woman shouting at the director. Yelling and anger always made Everett's stomach knot up. Absently he had rubbed slow circles on his midsection as he watched the pretty woman in the red shirt rush past Cora's desk.

Why did women always start shouting when they got upset? If they would only ask nicely, they might get whatever it was that they wanted.

No one ever seemed to notice Everett, so he was able to watch the other employees whenever he had a break from his work. Sometimes he was able to listen to their conversations, if they talked loud enough. It helped him to figure out why some people had so many friends and others, like him, didn't.

On a really good day, he would see Leslie Logan. She came often to Children's Connection, looking like a modern-day queen. Everett had a special reason for watching her, but it wasn't what anyone else might think. Leslie was old enough to be his mother.

Everett glanced at his watch and saw that it was time for him to get back to his desk before someone asked where he'd been. Nervously he pushed back his hair as he looked around to make sure that no one was watching him. The hall was empty and the pretty woman in red was gone. He was in the clear.

Two

Emma was still fuming over her appointment when she hurried to meet her friend Ivy Crosby for lunch at a little café near the computer company where Ivy worked. Even though her family owned Crosby Systems, Ivy never took for granted her position there, so Emma didn't want to be late and hold her up.

She could see Ivy already seated at one of the small tables outside the café, her curly blond hair easy to spot, even in the middle of the lunch-hour crowd. She smiled and waved when she saw Emma coming down the sidewalk.

Despite her own foul mood, Emma waved back before she ducked inside and worked her way through the groups of people waiting to be seated.

"I'm joining my friend at an outside table," she told the hostess.

Emma and Ivy had been roommates in college. Despite their polar-opposite personalities and wildly diverse backgrounds, they had made the effort to remain close.

When Emma got to the table, Ivy stood up and gave her a hug.

"I'm so glad to see you," Ivy exclaimed. "I missed you."

"You, too." Emma returned her hug, blinking back tears. "I'm glad you're back."

Ivy's perfume was a designer scent that cost more than Emma's laptop, or her trendy outfit from an exclusive boutique. Beneath the affluent veneer, Ivy was the most genuine and loyal friend Emma had.

"How have you been?" Ivy asked after they had both sat down. "Fill me in."

"Is there steam coming out of my ears?" Emma asked teasingly. Inwardly she was still fuming about her meeting.

Ivy's blue eyes widened as she folded her hands on the menu. "Oh, dear," she replied. "It sounds as if you've had a bad morning. Tell me what's wrong."

Emma was touched by her friend's concern, but she knew how much Ivy hated being late back to work. She said it set a bad example for the other employees. "My problems will keep. Let's order." She glanced at her menu. "Then I want to hear about your trip. Where was it again that you went?"

"Lantanya."

"I've never heard of it." Emma wondered if she had imagined the momentary coolness in Ivy's voice, even as the poetic name rolled off her tongue.

"No one has. It's just a tiny principality located right on the Adriatic Sea." She tossed her blond head. "Lunch is my treat. Don't even bother to argue."

Emma was embarrassed by Ivy's generosity, but she was too broke to protest. After they had both ordered seafood salad and iced tea, she managed to smile at her friend.

"Did you meet a handsome prince while you were in Lantanya?" Emma asked teasingly.

To her surprise, Ivy's expression froze. "I wasn't there to play," she said. "It was a business trip."

"I was only kidding," Emma replied, refusing to take offense. She was well aware of the stress Ivy felt when it came to her job. "So how was business?"

Ivy's face relaxed again. "Crosby Industries is putting computer systems in the schools there. The children are so excited. It's a heartwarming project."

When it came to kids, Ivy was a cream puff. A few months ago, she had started volunteering at Portland General, working with the crack babies.

"That sounds great," Emma replied. "Will you be going back?"

Again Ivy's smile wavered and she glanced away. "I doubt it."

"I suppose the country is pretty primitive," Emma said. "Is it hot and barren?"

Before Ivy could reply, the waitress brought their salads and tall glasses of iced tea.

"Anything else?" the young girl asked. When both of them shook their heads, she left the check on the table and departed.

"Lantanya is a lovely country," Ivy murmured, picking up her fork. "I've just had enough traveling for a while."

Something wasn't right here. In college the two girls had spent a lot of time talking about all the places they wanted to visit when they had an opportunity to travel. Before she left, Ivy had been eager to go on this trip.

Concerned, Emma leaned across the small table. "Honey, what's wrong? Did something happen while you were gone?"

To her dismay, tears swam in Ivy's eyes before she blinked them away. "I guess you could say that," she whispered. "I met someone."

Emma was probably the only person who knew just how inexperienced Ivy was when it came to men. "And?" she prompted.

"And we hit it off, and now it's over." Ivy's eyes were downcast as she speared a bite of her salad.

"I'm sorry." Emma was dying for more information, but it was obvious that Ivy wasn't ready to talk about whatever had taken place in Lantanya. For a few moments the two of them ate in silence.

Finally Ivy lifted her head, her smile firmly back in place. "Okay, no more stalling. When you first arrived, you looked fit to be tied, as my nanny used to say."

Ivy already knew about Emma's medical condition, her divorce from Don and her layoff. Emma hadn't yet mentioned her estrangement from the people who had raised her or the reason behind it.

As briefly as possible, Emma explained how finding out about her endometriosis had led to the news that she was adopted.

"I don't know what to say," Ivy murmured. "Are you sure it's true?"

Emma speared a fat pink shrimp, even though she wasn't at all hungry. The one good thing that had come out of the recent weeks was that she had lost a few pounds. "Mom admitted everything."

Ivy sprinkled pepper on her hard-boiled egg. Her own childhood had been less than ideal. She had been raised by a series of housekeepers and nannies after her parents' divorce, but at least Ivy knew who she was.

"I'm so sorry," she said with a sympathetic smile. "What they did was wrong, but they're good people at heart and they love you. I know you'll work it out."

"We're not speaking," Emma said bluntly as she poked at her salad. "I can't forgive them for lying to me all these years."

At the next table, a cell phone rang and the man sitting there launched into a loud, annoying conversation about a deal he was putting together.

Ivy rolled her eyes in reaction. "What exactly did your parents tell you?"

Emma arched her brows. "Do you mean the Wrights?" she asked, unable to resist.

After her divorce, she had taken back her maiden name. If she had known when she signed the papers what she knew now, she wouldn't have bothered.

"They're still your parents," Ivy chided gently before taking a dainty bite of arugula.

Emma didn't bother to argue. She couldn't expect her friend to understand her sense of betrayal. Ivy was under constant pressure working at the family firm, but at least they *were* her family.

Someone dropped a tray inside the café with a loud crash that made Emma's hand jerk. Iced tea sloshed over the rim of the glass.

"Did they tell you anything else about your background?" Ivy asked.

"Only that I was a newborn when they adopted me," Emma explained as she wiped up the spill with her napkin. "It was handled by an agency here in Portland called Children's Connection."

Blotting her lips with her napkin, Ivy studied her thoughtfully. "I've seen their ads. The Logans are big patrons of their fertility clinic."

Emma was aware that Ivy's family and the wealthy Logans had a long, mutually antagonistic history, but she wasn't sure why. Ivy had told her their companies were rivals, but the rift seemed far too bitter for that. "I'm sorry," she said. "I didn't know they were involved."

"No reason you should." Ivy studied her thoughtfully. "It's good to know the adoption was legitimate and not part of some backroom black-market baby ring."

"I guess," Emma acknowledged.

A sudden breeze stirred Ivy's hair. Two men at a nearby table stopped talking to stare at her. Despite being so pretty, she had been raised in the shadow of her older siblings, which made her rather shy. She was oblivious to the men's attention.

"I don't know what I'd do if I found out something like that," she told Emma. "Is that where you went this morning?"

Emma leaned closer and lowered her voice. Thankfully the hotshot at the next table had concluded his call and was eating his lunch. "I had an appointment with the director, because I wanted to learn everything I could about my biological parents."

Ivy set aside her plate. "I guess I'd want to know the same thing. What did you find out?"

"Nothing!" Emma's frustration bubbled out. Several patrons glanced over at her, so she quickly lowered her voice. "He refused to tell me anything. He claimed that my file is confidential."

"Well, maybe it's for the best," Ivy said in a concil-iatory tone. "I mean, are you sure you *really* want to know the reasons someone gave you up? What if they're painful?"

"Like what?" Emma fired back at her. "You mean, if my mother was too young to take care of me, or if I was the result of some kind of assault or incest, or left in a Dumpster?" She had already spent a lot of time think-ing about all the different possibilities.

Ivy shrugged. "I don't know. Some people don't want anyone to find out they had a child and gave it up. They're ashamed, or they have a new family they never told. Or they just can't face what they did."

"I still have a right to know," Emma disagreed. "It's my personal history." She could feel the frustration ris-ing up again, but the last thing she wanted was to argue with Ivy.

"But you said they couldn't tell you anything, so what else can you do?"

"I said they *wouldn't* tell me," Emma corrected. "The director, Morgan Davis, had my file with the names of my parents right on his desk. He admitted the informa-tion was all there, but it's agency policy to keep it all a big, dark secret."

She took a gulp of her iced tea, but the ice had melted and it tasted watery. "You'd think this was the nineteenth century, not the twenty-first," she sputtered. "Adoption files have been open for decades!"

Ivy took out her wallet and put her credit card with the check. "Do you want to take a walk?" she offered. "I could use the exercise."

A knot rose up in Emma's throat at her friend's suggestion. "Thanks for letting me vent, sweetie. I know you need to get back to work." She glanced at her watch. "Don't worry. I'll be okay."

"Any job leads?" Ivy asked after the waitress went off with her card.

Emma had to be careful not to say too much about that situation, because she knew Ivy would repeat her offer to find Emma something at Crosby Systems. Even though Ivy's family owned the business and her older brother was the CEO, she wanted to be seen there as more than a pretty face. She had struggled hard for the recognition she had achieved and Emma was determined not to impose on their friendship.

"I'm looking into a couple of things for fall," she said with a smile. "Meanwhile I've got my part-time job at the video store and my unemployment benefits, so I'm not concerned."

She might have been able to squeak along for a while if Don hadn't left her with more than her share of their bills. Contrary to what she had just told Ivy, she was starting to worry about how she was going to manage.

"Promise you'll let me know if I can help," Ivy said, touching Emma's hand. "I'm serious. Give me your word."

Crossing the fingers of her other hand beneath the table, Emma nodded. "I know one of my leads will pan out anyday."

"And I'm so sorry about this other business," Ivy said after she'd tucked her credit card back into her purse and they wound their way out of the café. "I'm sure not knowing is hard, but it sounds as if you have no choice but to let it go."

The two of them stopped on the sidewalk to exchange a quick hug. "Call me whenever you feel like talking, okay?"

Once again Emma nodded. "Same goes, you know."

Ivy's cheeks turned pink, but she didn't reply.

"Well, thanks for listening," Emma told her, "and for lunch." As soon as she landed a full-time job and got caught up on her bills, she was going to take Ivy to dinner at the nicest restaurant in Portland as thanks for her support.

"Anytime." With a final wave, Ivy turned and walked quickly away.

Emma hesitated, not sure what to do next. The rest of the afternoon stretched in front of her like an empty road. After the way her morning had gone, she deserved a treat. Something more lasting than lunch.

One of her favorite places to go in downtown Portland was a bookstore named Powell's. Housed in a big old building, it was known as the largest independent new and used bookstore in the world. Maybe a couple of hours spent perusing the shelves would take her mind off that jerk, Morgan Davis.

After a solitary lunch at his desk, a staff meeting and an appointment with an eager couple looking to adopt a baby, Morgan took time to double-check his vacation plans. Every summer, aided by grants and donations, he and a group of volunteers conducted a two-week summer camp in the mountains a couple of hours away from the city.

The camp session was for older children who were still waiting to be adopted. It was Morgan's way of reminding them that people cared, of giving back to a system that had changed his life. The setting, on a lakeshore in the Deschutes National Forest, never failed to renew his spirit.

As usual, most of the office staff was already gone by the time he'd returned a list of phone calls and cleared off his desk. Even Cora had finally stuck her head in the doorway to see if there was anything he needed before she left to pick up her children from day care.

He walked to his reserved parking spot a few minutes later, carrying the briefcase that had been a birthday gift from his parents. In deference to the lingering heat, he had tossed the jacket of his suit over his shoulder and loosened his Italian silk tie.

He was aware that some of his staff members thought he overdressed for the job, but the responsibility of his position as the director weighed heavily on his shoulders. His goal was to present an image of reassurance and responsibility in order to gain people's trust. He had helped to build Children's Connection into a nationally known and respected agency. Every year they helped hundreds of people to attain their dream of having a family.

He was proud of the work they did. That was why cases like Emma Wright's weighed heavily on his mind.

Meanwhile Morgan's parents were visiting from California for a few days. As usual, they'd refused his offer of the guest room at his condo, preferring to stay at a nearby hotel instead.

"Packing it in, Mr. D?" asked the parking guard as Morgan unlocked the door to his sensible SUV.

"Figured it was time, Andy," he replied. "How's your wife's foot? Is she feeling better?"

Andy had mentioned that she'd tripped over a grand-child's toy truck a couple of days before.

"Getting better," he said now. "Thanks for asking, though." He ran his hand through his tightly curled gray hair. "Enjoy your evening."

Morgan's mother claimed they didn't want to "upset his routine" by staying with him, but he suspected an ulterior motive. She made no secret of her desire for a passel of grandbabies to spoil. To that end, she wasn't about to invade his privacy, just in case he had a girl-friend tucked away.

He would like nothing better than to enjoy a serious relationship with a woman he could picture spending his life with, but so far it hadn't happened. Perhaps he was foolish to believe that he would somehow know when he met the one meant for him—that special woman—but he wasn't willing to settle for less. Meanwhile, he was busy with the agency, the summer camp and the occasional date with a potential soul mate.

His town house was part of a fairly new complex located a few miles from the office. It had a great view of the Willamette River. Despite the heavy rush-hour traffic that streamed from downtown Portland to the suburbs, his commute took less than a half hour, giving him plenty of time to shower and change clothes before meeting his folks for dinner.

"You seem preoccupied," Morgan's mother said after the waiter left with their orders. "Did something happen at work today?"

He glanced at his father, a pediatrician he respected more than any man he'd ever known.

"Might as well tell her," Dr. Davis suggested with a grin. "She's like one of those California condors. She won't rest until she's picked you clean."

Morgan's mother, a teacher, swatted at him with her napkin. The love between the two of them never failed to strengthen his own determination to find that one special woman with whom he could form a similar bond.

"I met someone today." He knew his mother would pounce on his comment like a duck on a bug.

Hazel eyes widening below her silver bangs, she leaned forward eagerly. "Really?"

"Don't tease her, son," his father said dryly.

A wave of remorse washed over Morgan. He was well aware that what she and his father wanted—all they had ever wanted—was his happiness.

And a few grandbabies to spoil, of course.

"It's not what you think, Mom," he cautioned as the waiter brought their drinks. "This woman recently found out she was adopted through Children's Connection and she was looking for answers."

His father frowned thoughtfully. "Were you able to help her?" he asked in the calm voice that had reassured thousands of young patients through the course of his medical career.

Morgan fiddled with the stem of his wine goblet as he pictured Emma's face, her sooty eyes swimming with tears. He should have tried harder to soften her disappointment.

"Well, Emma did slam the door to my office pretty hard when she left," he admitted wryly, sitting back in his chair when the waiter brought their salads. "I'd take that as a no."

The waiter's expression didn't alter as he offered each of them fresh-ground pepper. He must overhear some interesting bits of conversation during a shift, Morgan thought.

"Was Emma pretty?" His mother's gaze gleamed with interest.

"What did she want to know?" his father asked at the same time.

"She's extremely pretty." Morgan pictured her in his mind. "Her hair is brown and wavy. She's got big gray eyes that a man could get lost in."

Too late he realized he'd said too much, so he focused on his salad.

"Is that all?" his father asked.

"Is she single?" His mother's expression was eager enough to make Morgan nervous.

"Legs that won't quit and curves in all the right places," he added for his father's benefit. "Divorced," he admitted to his mother.

As long as he didn't divulge Emma's full name, he wasn't technically breaching confidentiality. Unless, of course, they started dating and she met his folks. Then he would have to tell her what he'd done, but what were the odds he would ever see her again?

"And?" his mother gestured with her fork.

"She's just lost her job as a school counselor," he blurted out.

"That sounds like a lot for a young woman to deal with." His father's voice was sympathetic.

"You find a woman with a problem more attractive than one wearing a thong bikini," his mother commented.

Morgan's mouth dropped open. "Excuse me?"

She peered at him through her glasses. "You're a sucker for a woman who needs help."

"Stella, let the boy eat," his father said with a wink at Morgan. "We're not going to marry him off tonight."

"I was raised by a doctor and a teacher," Morgan drawled. "I'd say that helping people runs in the family."

For a few moments, conversation lagged as the three of them ate their salads. Silently Morgan reviewed in his mind everything Emma had told him. With a sigh of regret, he arrived at the same conclusion as before—that there was nothing else he could have done without compromising the agency's rules and his own principles, as well as adding to the burden of heartbreak she already appeared to carry.

"What do you think of the Trailblazers' prospects?" Dr. Davis asked. Portland boasted an NBA basketball team, but the closest thing to major league baseball was a Triple-A team named the Beavers.

"Too soon to tell," Morgan replied. Even though he wasn't really a Blazers fan, he was grateful for the change of subject.

His mother didn't mention Emma again. After dinner he kissed his mother's cheek and shook his father's hand.

"Keep us posted on your progress," she said with a wink.

"Don't start knitting booties yet," he replied before heading back to his condo.

In the solitude of his home office, he kicked off his

shoes and thought again about getting a dog. It would be alone while he worked, of course, but the idea of some living being getting excited over his arrival had a certain appeal.

With the stereo playing softly, he reviewed a research report from a fertility clinic on the East Coast, read the files of two candidates for his summer camp program and frowned over a rate increase submitted by the agency's Web site designer.

After he had loaded the paperwork back into his briefcase, he poured himself a glass of wine. He wasn't an expert, but it was a pleasing vintage by an Oregon grower. He popped Placido Domingo's latest CD into the player. Neither was he a real opera buff, but he'd been a fan of the Italian singer since accompanying a friend to a 3 Tenors concert in San Francisco.

As the notes from a haunting ballad filled the room, Morgan propped his stocking feet on the coffee table and tipped back his head, attempting to empty his mind. Placido might not have been pleased to know that it was Emma Wright's voice that echoed through Morgan's head as the twilight glowing through the windows dimmed, leaving the room in shadows. He contemplated switching on the brass lamp at his elbow, but the deepening gloom suited his mood.

During his years at Children's Connection, he'd heard more hard luck stories than he could count. He'd seen infertility overcome, families formed and empty hearts—big and small—filled with love.

Of course, not everyone left happy. Some problems couldn't be cured. Some people didn't qualify for adoption, some children grew from cuddly to surly without being placed. Morgan ached for them all.

He swallowed the last of the Merlot in his glass and thought of Emma—not what he couldn't do, but what he might do.

The answer was so simple that he nearly laughed aloud. From what she had told him, names were only one of the things she needed. Morgan could put a little money in her pocket without getting slapped for his trouble, while at the same time he solved a problem of his own.

A couple of days after her lunch with Ivy, Emma drove down to the office of a school district in the Willamette Valley near Eugene for an interview. After her talk with the superintendent, she suspected the trip to be a waste of her time and gas, her appointment a formality and the position already earmarked for a candidate within the district. The only thing she'd learned from the trip was that her car was going to need new struts in the very near future.

When Emma got back to her apartment complex, she parked in her assigned slot and retrieved the mail from her box in the central kiosk. As she walked back across the asphalt, she shuffled through the bills, junk mail and sale flyers. The hot afternoon sun seemed to soak right through her navy cotton dress. Without water, the surrounding lawn had dried until it looked like shredded wheat and the few spindly trees provided only a thimble's worth of shade.

Ignoring the peeling paint on the front door of her unit, she let herself inside. The blinds were closed against the sunlight, so the temperature was slightly less than a warming oven. The message light on her answering machine was flashing, but she ignored it as she bent to pet her cat, a recent shelter survivor named Posy.

"Hi, baby," Emma crooned as the fluffy Siamese-Himalayan mix kitten entwined itself around her ankles.

Posy's response to being roused from her nap was a soulful plea for attention and fresh food, not necessarily in that order.

As Emma scratched beneath the kitty's chin, she couldn't help but wonder just how much longer she'd be able to afford this place, cheap though it was. Since the school district had let her go, she had been working in a nearby video store. The pay was abysmal, the blare of the soundtracks annoying, and the endless task of restocking the rentals mind numbing to the extreme.

The manager appeared young enough to be carded every time he ordered a drink. Just the other day he had told Emma that her hours would be cut at the end of August to make room for the returning college crew.

She would need to look for something else to supplement her dwindling funds until she lined up a fall job, she thought grimly as she filled Posy's water dish. The two of them would end up on the streets before Emma would consider asking her adoptive parents for a loan.

She didn't listen to the message on her machine until she got back from work with an old Mel Gibson movie under her arm. She had spent her evening unpacking and logging in the latest new DVDs—a gory-looking slasher film, an action sequel about a mutant and a romantic comedy with stars who appeared young enough to be shopping for back-to-school supplies. Listening to her co-worker gush about the male lead made Emma feel old.

The phone message was from her adoptive mother, Sally Wright. Her plaintive tone made Emma's heart ache until she reminded herself that *she* was the innocent victim. The Wrights were more concerned with sweeping the entire issue beneath the carpet and pretending that none of it had ever happened than in trying to understand Emma's desperate need to find her roots.

As Emma slid the tape into her aging VCR and sat down on the couch with her cat, she felt as though there was a yawning hole inside her where the knowledge of family used to be. Until she figured out how to fill it back up, she had no idea what to say if Sally called again. Emma's feelings were still too raw. If the phone rang while Emma was home, there was always Caller ID.

"Are you sure you don't have personal reasons for wanting to offer her the job?" asked Aaron Levy, Morgan's neighbor, as the two of them pounded down the pathway along the riverbank.

Aaron was an attorney with a social conscience and a trust fund. He practiced out of a storefront law office in an older part of downtown Portland. He and Morgan made a point to run together before work whenever their schedules permitted.

Aaron was training for an upcoming marathon, and Morgan, who wasn't a serious runner, had foolishly agreed to go the extra distance with him. Morgan was saved from finding the breath to reply as they crossed the common area surrounding their building.

They pulled up, Morgan gasping. "Like I told you," he said, panting, his heart thudding like the drum in a marching band, "I feel sorry for her."

Aaron didn't appear to be breathing hard, but his laughter was still uneven.

"Be careful, my friend," he warned, bending over. "That's what I told myself about my ex."

Morgan used his damp T-shirt to mop the perspiration from his face. "I didn't know you'd been married."

Straightening back up, Aaron shrugged. "It only lasted long enough for me to realize that pity isn't a substitute for love." He twisted his torso and stretched from the waist. He was a vegetarian and as whipcord lean as a greyhound.

"I don't love Emma," Morgan protested, alarmed by the attorney's assumption. "I don't even know her."

He didn't want to go into her whole story as he'd

done with his parents, so all he had said was that he'd met her and she needed a boost.

"I like helping people," he added, wincing at the defensiveness in his tone.

True to form, Aaron heard it, too. "Careful, man." A grin broke on his long, homely face as he started backing away. "Your words say 'no, no,' but your eyes say 'let's get naked.'"

With a laugh, Morgan waved him off. "That's your fantasy, not mine."

"And a great fantasy it is," Aaron called after him. "When you're picking out the ring, just remember that I warned you, and don't hit me up to be best man."

Morgan ignored his last comment, but a few minutes later when he was standing under the hot blast of the shower, his mind veered to it. Was his brainstorm just a flimsy excuse to see her again?

As he toweled himself dry, he didn't waste time analyzing his motives. His parents hadn't raised him to put his own selfish needs first. Other people counted on him and he didn't let them down.

Wrapping the towel around his waist, he walked into his bedroom. This morning he paid no attention to the soothing shades of pearl gray and charcoal as he finished dressing. He was in a sudden hurry to get to work.

Emma had stayed up late watching movies, and the next morning the phone woke her. As she rolled over to grab the receiver, not yet awake enough to think about screening the call, Posy protested from her nest behind the bend of Emma's knees.

"Hold on for a minute, okay?" Emma told the cat. "Hello?"

Silence greeted her. The telemarketers must be starting early. The clock by her bed said it was barely past nine.

"Hello?" she said again, some of her surliness over being woken up leaking into her tone.

"Emma Wright?"

She didn't immediately recognize the voice, but it sounded familiar. Maybe it was a callback about a job interview.

She sat up straighter, wishing she had some water as she consciously sweetened her tone. "This is Emma." With her free hand, she patted Posy so the cat would be quiet.

"I'm sorry to bother you," the man's voice continued. "I, um, didn't mean to disturb you."

Damn, he could tell she was still in bed. Emma's cheeks grew hot at the idea that he'd probably heard her comment to Posy and assumed Emma wasn't alone.

"No, no, it's okay," she replied eagerly. "You didn't bother me at all. How can I help you?" She still couldn't place the voice, but if it turned out to be a salesman on the other end of the line, she was going to be really, really annoyed.

"This is Morgan Davis from Children's Connection," he said. "We met the other day."

Emma nearly dropped the receiver and the muscles of her throat closed so tight that she could hardly croak out a reply.

"Did you change your mind?" she asked.

"About what?" He sounded puzzled.

"My parents' identity," she replied. "Why else would you call me?"

When she heard him sigh, her heart plummeted.

"I'm sorry," he said. "I thought I made it clear that your file is confidential and there's nothing I can do."

She pushed her hair back from her face, fully awake now. If this was a personal call, she was going to slap him with a harassment suit for getting her hopes up.

"What, you had to call in case I didn't get that already?" she snapped. "You and I have nothing else to discuss!"

"Please don't hang up," he said quickly. "The reason I'm calling is to offer you a job."

Three

Morgan Davis had said the magic word. *Job*. It was the only thing that prevented Emma's hand from slamming down the receiver. Her cat leaped down from the bed with obvious annoyance, tail twitching.

"What do you have in mind?" Emma asked cautiously.

The director of Children's Connection hadn't struck her as a player, despite his awesome appearance. He'd been totally businesslike, but a woman couldn't be too careful and Emma had been wrong before. If he suggested they meet somewhere cozy—like a bar—to discuss it, she was definitely hanging up.

"Let me explain," he replied. "Every year a group of us takes two weeks of our vacation time in August to put on a camp session for some of the kids who haven't yet been placed with adoptive families," he replied. "Everyone pitches in wherever we're needed. It's a lot of fun."

"How would this apply to me?" she asked as soon as she realized that he was talking about volunteering. Since she'd told him she had lost her job, he probably figured she wasn't working at all and had a lot of time. She didn't have that luxury; even the video store job put a little money in her pocket.

Before she could refuse, he began talking again.

"With your background as a school counselor, you'd be a great addition." His voice was filled with enthusiasm. "I know it's just temporary, but we're funded by grants and donations, so we do have a small budget. In addition to getting room and board for two weeks, you'd be paid a salary."

She would have expected it to be a fraction of what he said, but it was more than she earned at her part-time job. They must have a generous benefactor.

"When does it start?" she asked.

He cleared his throat. "Next week. Sorry for the late notice. I hope it will work out for you. Someone else backed out—broke her leg in a boating accident—so a spot opened up."

"As a counselor?" she asked.

"Uh, partly."

His suddenly evasive tone made her curious. "And what else?"

"How do you feel about peeling potatoes?" he asked with an edge of humor. "She was also going to help out the cook."

Posy hopped back onto the bed and butted Emma's hand.

"Hey, baby," Emma cooed, patting her silky fur. "Looking for attention?"

"Look, I'm obviously interrupting something," the voice over the phone said hastily. "Why don't you think it over and get back to me. Just tell Cora that I'm expecting your call."

His sudden abruptness puzzled Emma. Before she could say anything, Posy apparently got tired of waiting for breakfast. She let out a yowl of displeasure as only a Siamese could, right into the receiver.

"I hope that didn't destroy your eardrums," Emma said quickly as she pushed Posy away.

"Was that a cat?" He sounded startled. Maybe he didn't like animals.

"Yeah. I think she's hungry."

The richness of his chuckle surprised Emma again. "I thought— Well, never mind what I thought."

His voice had shifted, becoming huskier and definitely more human. The image of his face, tan complexion, dark hair and blue eyes flashed across her consciousness as the intimacy of his tone sent shivers down her bare arms.

Her hand tightened on the receiver as suddenly it dawned on her why he hadn't finished voicing his assumption. He could tell that she'd been asleep when he called. He'd overheard her comment to her cat and assumed she was making pillow talk with a lover!

Emma couldn't decide whether to be flattered or embarrassed, but her free hand tugged automatically on the neckline of her nightie, making sure she was decently covered.

"Where's the camp session going to be held?" she asked.

"It's in a fantastic place called Camp Baxter in the Cascade foothills. We lease their facility every year."

"I've heard of it, but I've never been there," she replied. "I'm not really an outdoorsy kind of person." Roughing it in the great outdoors had never attracted her, and being a contestant on *Survivor* was her worst nightmare. She was too fond of her creature comforts—not that she'd be able to afford them for much longer if she didn't get a steady job.

"We'll change that." His voice was full of confidence.

Maybe she didn't *want* that part of her changed. Being pampered was way more appealing than sleeping on a bed of pine cones and rushes.

"I don't know—"

"Why don't you mull over the idea and give me a call

back, today or tomorrow if you can?" he suggested. "The kids you'll be working with are terrific. You'll love them. We bus them out there, and the rest of the staff takes a van."

"If I can find someone to cat-sit, I'll do it," Emma said, going totally on impulse.

It wasn't the idea of fresh air that attracted her, it was getting a second chance with the person who held the key to her genealogy!

"Are you sure?" He must have been a little taken aback by her quick acceptance.

"Yes," she replied, thinking fast. Even though he had been the one to call her, the last thing she wanted was to make him suspicious. "It would be a great addition to my résumé," she added.

"Well, that's probably true. Why don't you deal with the cat and let me know for sure?"

As soon as she agreed and ended the call, Emma bolted for the bathroom. That would teach her to drink a soda right before bedtime.

"Of course I'll feed your cat," Ivy said, "but I wish you'd reconsider the entire idea."

The two friends were sitting on Emma's old couch sharing a pizza that Ivy had brought with her. Emma was beginning to wish that she hadn't told Ivy about her plan to persuade the director to change his mind and let her see her file. Thank goodness she hadn't confided her entire scheme. For someone who had grown up rich, Ivy could be remarkably naive and easily shocked.

"I've struck out in trying to find my parents' names through any other source," Emma said around a mouthful of pepperoni pizza. "This guy is my last hope."

"Maybe your parents—" At Emma's glare, Ivy shook her head. "Pardon me. Maybe your *adoptive* parents had the right idea when they asked you to put it behind you so you can move on," she continued.

Before Emma could interrupt, Ivy put a hand on her arm. "Hear me out, okay?"

Emma nodded, frustrated, and tore off another bite of pizza. Ivy's upbringing had been far from ordinary, but she didn't seem to understand Emma's determination. This could very well be her only opportunity to solve the mystery of her past.

"You said this guy Morgan is really attractive, right?" Ivy asked. "And he doesn't wear a wedding ring, so he's probably not married."

"Lots of guys don't—"

Ivy ignored Emma's interruption. "What if your plan to get on his good side backfires? I mean, what if he's single and you get to know him really well? What if he's a great guy and you end up falling for him?"

"That's not going to happen!" Emma huffed. She didn't need that kind of complication right now.

"You're completely over Don, right?" Ivy asked after she'd taken a ladylike sip of her soda.

"Need you ask?" Emma rolled her eyes. "Toad-boy deserted me when I needed him. He stopped loving me—if he ever did to start with—because of something that wasn't my fault."

Just thinking about her ex-husband was enough to destroy Emma's appetite. What had she ever seen in him? Why had she wanted *children* with him?

Angrily she set aside her paper plate. "I am so over that creep that I hope I never see his face again."

"See?" Ivy exclaimed. "You're emotionally vulnerable. Spending two weeks in close quarters with the new hunk could get complicated, especially the kind of hunk who might be the total opposite of toad-boy."

"How so?" Emma patted the couch cushion.

Posy jumped up between them and settled down with her front paws tucked under her fluffy fur.

"Well, it sounds like he's kindhearted as well as cute," Ivy replied as she held out her fingers for the cat to sniff.

"Kindhearted?" Emma echoed. "I don't think so. Remember how Mr. Kindness treated me?"

"Maybe so, but anyone willing to give up prime August vacation time for a group of orphans must have a *few* noble qualities," Ivy retorted.

"I'm not attracted to him," Emma insisted. If she were Pinocchio, her nose would have provided them both with firewood for the winter. Under very different circumstances, she *might* have been interested.

"I wish you'd reconsider," Ivy said, blotting her

mouth with a napkin. "I'm not saying that you shouldn't go, because I think the break would do you good. Spending time with nature can be a healing experience."

She ignored Emma's derisive snort. Outdoor plumbing and bug bites didn't sound very healing to her!

"You won't accept a loan from me," Ivy continued, "so I can't, in good conscience, advise you to turn this down. I just wish you'd forget the idea of trying to manipulate him into going against the rules."

Unless Emma agreed, they weren't going to have time to watch the latest Brad Pitt movie, and she had to return it tomorrow. "I'll think about what you said," she conceded reluctantly.

Maybe Ivy was right and Emma's scheme was beyond ridiculous, but she had to do something to put her life back on track. Other than landing a great job so she could get caught up on the bills, she just wasn't sure where to start.

Most of the staff rode to camp in a van, but Morgan liked to accompany the kids, nearly thirty of them this year. He rode in the bus.

The trip to the site near the Deschutes National Forest in central Oregon took about three hours. That was plenty of time for Morgan to renew friendships with the kids who'd attended last year's session, to start sizing up the new kids and to mentally begin pairing them off.

After a round of introductions, he led them in camp

songs until his throat hurt. With each passing mile, he could feel his personal stress melting away. Sometimes people asked how he could give up the chance to spend his vacation in Hawaii or Mexico, but more than anywhere else in the world, Camp Baxter held a special place in his heart.

The bus signaled to pull off the road at a rest area so they could use the facilities and eat their sack lunches. The van that followed behind them carried the ice chest full of cold drinks. The cook and one of the helpers had gone up earlier with the rest of the supplies.

He wondered if Emma Wright would find the forest of soaring firs and the deep lake as breathtaking as he always did. She had sounded like a real tenderfoot on the phone and she hadn't said much when they all met in the hospital parking lot with their duffels and sleeping bags this morning.

Since she was the only newcomer, he had introduced her to the others. Before he could offer to help with her gear, Jeff, a male nurse at Portland General, took the opportunity to show off his muscles. The spurt of possessiveness Morgan felt when he watched her smile at Jeff had caught him off guard.

Now Morgan lurched to his feet as the bus braked to a stop. "Okay, kids, stay in your seats until I tell you to get up, okay?" he said.

"I gotta *go!*" a young boy shouted, followed by a chorus of "Me, too. Me, too."

Morgan ducked down to look out the window and see if the van had arrived. He'd learned the hard way not to turn the kids loose until the reinforcements had arrived, or they would scatter like spilled buckshot in a munitions factory.

To his relief, the van pulled up right next to them. No doubt the rest of the staff members were also grateful for the pit stop, especially the ones who had begun the trip carrying large coffee mugs from Starbucks. People in the northwest loved their coffee.

He nodded to the driver, who opened the door. After Morgan had descended the steps first, he helped the younger passengers out. His assistants quickly separated the boys and girls into two groups and led them away.

"No running!" Heidi called out. She was a caseworker, too, and her husband, Derrick, was in the second year of his residency at Portland General. Between him, Jeff and those who were Red Cross certified, there would be no shortage of trained medical personnel.

Emma, wearing denim cutoffs and a plaid blouse, was the last to exit the van. Jeff helped her down, saying something that made her laugh before he, too, hurried toward the long, low main building.

When her gaze met Morgan's, she surprised him by smiling before she donned blue-tinted sunglasses. After her outburst back in his office the first time they had met, he hadn't been sure what to expect, despite her civility on the phone.

One of the female college students waited for Emma to join her.

"Doing okay?" Morgan asked the two of them.

"I can't wait to get there," Franny replied.

Emma merely nodded before Franny gestured toward the facilities and the two of them walked away together. In a few moments, the kids would be coming back to the picnic tables, so Morgan took advantage of the break as well.

"He's so cute," Franny said under her breath as she and Emma hurried down the path. "Don't you think so?"

Except for Morgan, the bus driver and the two staffers who had driven over earlier, everyone else was riding together in the van. The five others already knew each other and they had all been at the camp before. Franny and another girl, Sarah, had made a special point of including Emma in the lively conversation.

Emma would have liked to ignore Franny's question about Morgan, but she didn't want to appear unfriendly.

"I consider any man with black hair and blue eyes to be attractive," she replied, attempting to sound flip as they joined the line on the ladies' side of the concrete building.

Fifteen young girls from the bus were ahead of them. A few of them chatted and giggled, one or two squirmed impatiently and the rest stood in silence with arms folded and their heads bowed.

Morgan had warned Emma that most of these kids

had never been placed, for one reason or another. The rest were here because of disrupted adoptions, ones that hadn't worked out.

She couldn't imagine how awful it would feel to get sent back, no matter what the reason. After dealing with that kind of rejection, these kids weren't about to risk it again.

"Were you talking about Morgan?" Sarah asked, sticking her head around the open rest room door as she wiped her hands. "For an older guy, he's not bad."

"Jeez, how old is he?" Emma asked with a lift of her eyebrows. Compared to these girls, she must, at twenty-seven, seem like Methuselah's sister.

Sarah shrugged her narrow shoulders. She was fashionably thin with streaked hair and a silver ring piercing one side of her nose. "He's not *ancient,* but I heard someone say that he's over thirty."

"Good thing we all know CPR," Emma quipped.

"That's for sure," said a familiar masculine voice from behind them. "With some of us approaching senility, you never know when you'll need it."

How much of their conversation had Morgan heard? As Emma's face began to burn with embarrassment, Sarah and Franny turned around and burst into giggles.

"You're not that old," Sarah cooed as she made a point to look him up and down. "You've probably got a few miles left on you."

Emma realized right then that she probably wasn't

going to like Sarah very much. And Morgan looked totally different than he had at his office.

After seeing his banker attire of suit and tie, Emma would have guessed his idea of casual to be pleated khakis with a crease and a name-brand polo. Instead he wore old jeans and a faded USC T-shirt. She wondered if that was where he'd gone to school.

Even his expression appeared more relaxed as his sapphire eyes gleamed with humor. A dimple winked in one dark cheek.

Suddenly Emma recalled Ivy's comment. *What if...you end up falling for him?* That hadn't seemed like much of a threat, but now that he'd morphed into Personality Guy, she'd have to watch it.

The line moved forward as two young girls came out of the rest room. When they saw Morgan, they both blushed and started to giggle. One of them, who appeared to be about twelve, puffed out her flat chest, threw back her head and gave Morgan a look that could only be described as flirtatious.

His return smile was nearly paternal.

After the girls had walked back up the path, his gaze slid to Emma's. A muscle jumped in his cheek.

"Some of these kids will do just about anything for attention," he muttered sadly. "It should make for an interesting session."

She didn't want to know that he was compassionate and understanding, she thought sourly as she traipsed after four of the younger girls to the picnic tables a few minutes later. It was far easier to see Morgan as a stuffy and unbending jerk.

Right now the jerk was handing out cups of juice to go with the sack lunches each of their charges was opening. He must have said something funny, because a few of the kids laughed. Heidi was grinning, and her husband slapped Morgan's shoulder.

Silently Emma agreed with him that it was going to be an interesting couple of weeks—but for different reasons than he thought.

"How are you doing so far?" Derrick asked, handing her a sack lunch. He was one of those ordinary-looking guys whose face lit up when he smiled. So far he'd smiled a lot.

"Fine, thanks," Emma replied. She noticed that instead of claiming their own table, the adults were all sitting with the kids.

"Mind if I sit next to you?" she asked a little girl who seemed to be alone. "I'm Emma."

The child looked up at her through glasses with thick lenses. A corner of the frame had been mended with tape, and a pink birthmark marred her cheek.

"Sure," she said with a shy smile as she slid over to make room. "My name is Emily."

Morgan handed each of them a cup of apple juice. He leaned down and winked at Emily.

"Keep an eye on her," he whispered, indicating

Emma with his thumb. "She looks like the type who would grab your sandwich when you're not looking."

Emily giggled as she studied Emma. "I think she's pretty."

"So do I," Morgan whispered loudly, eliciting more giggles from Emily and a blush from Emma.

Between bites of the PB&J sandwich, Emma managed to introduce Emily to another girl who was sitting across from them. Petie jabbered like a magpie, but by the time she and Emily had finished their carrot sticks and cookies, a friendship was beginning to form. Emma hoped she wouldn't drop Emily as soon as she found other friends.

"That was nicely done," Morgan commented as Emma helped to make sure everyone took their trash to the receptacles.

"I do have a little experience with kids," she reminded him. "Grade school's my specialty."

Did the man miss nothing? He hadn't even been seated at their table. "Do you have eyes in the back of your head?" she couldn't resist asking him.

Again his dimple flashed when he grinned. "That's what some of the kids think," he drawled, "but I'll never tell."

"Morgan!" shouted the man driving the bus, jabbing a finger at his watch. "Time to head out."

Upon arrival at Camp Baxter, Emma helped out wherever she was needed, which seemed to be everywhere at once. Despite the obvious organization, there was a lot to accomplish before dark.

Assignment sheets and daily schedules were passed out to the staff. After the kids were divided among five cabins according to age and sex, the names of secret pals were distributed. The salad, chili and pans of cornbread prepared by Cookie were consumed down to the last crumb and kidney bean. As darkness fell, everyone sat around the fire pit for a sing-along and marshmallow roast.

Emma sat next to Petie and Emily, directly across from Morgan. After his welcoming speech, he surprised her with a string of corny jokes that destroyed the last bits of the image she'd had of him. They cracked some of the remaining ice in the group, too.

In the firelight he was so attractive when he grinned at Emma that she had to look away. After that, she was careful to watch everyone else except him.

Heidi and Derrick led the group in singing a couple of the silly songs, which provided a good diversion for Emma. The campfire songs reminded Emma of her Girl Scout troop. When the leader quit, Sally Wright had stepped in, despite having no experience, so the girls could stay together. Had Emma ever thanked her for that?

By the time she crawled into the sleeping bag on her cot that night, she was exhausted. The main lodge was a rather primitive log structure with plumbing facilities and a phone line, but no electricity. In Emma's eyes, her tiny private room was still infinitely better than bunking with a cabin full of hyperexcited young campers.

Franny and Sarah each slept with a group of girls. Jeff, along with the bus driver, whose name was Frank, and Mohammed, who had ridden up with the cook, were in charge of the boys. Morgan and Cookie each had rooms at the lodge. Heidi and Derrick shared, of course.

Although Emma had been warned about early reveille in the morning, she had trouble falling asleep. She tried thinking about her duties the next day, conducting craft projects, helping in the kitchen and making herself available in case anyone wanted to talk. Despite her best efforts, her mind, like a boomerang, kept returning to Morgan and his transformation.

She could see him as he acted out the words to "The Wheels on the Bus" at the campfire. His clowning had caught her by surprise.

Which was the real Morgan Davis—the stuffy director in the gray suit or the unselfconscious camp leader whose goal was to bring smiles to a circle of children? Emma's last thought before she finally drifted off to sleep was that getting to know him might be more interesting than she'd originally thought.

Everett felt as though everyone in the hospital cafeteria was staring at him as he stood in front of the vending machine looking for an empty table. His hands were damp with perspiration and he worried about dropping his tray.

He had done that once. It made a huge noise when it hit the floor, splattering his soup across the vinyl. For two weeks afterward, Everett had brought a sack lunch to work and eaten alone at his desk. Now he was careful to hold his tray tightly and not bump into anyone.

He'd thought the pretty nurse, Nancy Allen, might be here. He'd been working so hard that he had lost track of the time and now it was late enough for the lunch rush to be over.

A cafeteria worker was wiping off the empty tables. Employees were supposed to bus their own dishes, but not everyone did. Everett found that annoying. Rules were made for a reason. If no one followed them, there would be chaos.

Disappointed that he had missed seeing Nancy, he ignored the view from tall windows that opened onto the meditation garden. Instead he set his tray down on a clean table facing the doorway. He probably should have e-mailed her, but he didn't want to come across as pushy in case she was only being polite. She seemed to like him, but maybe she didn't want to hurt his feelings.

He stared down at the food in front of him. Lasagna was served every Thursday and he always selected it, just as he always had chicken on Mondays. Routine made him comfortable. He didn't like surprises. A person couldn't prepare for things if he didn't know what was going to happen.

Feeling a little anxious, Everett arranged the plates

of food in front of him. Once they were the way he liked, he opened the book he'd brought with him and began to eat. He was halfway through his lasagna when the sound of voices distracted him from the mystery he was reading.

He lifted his head, immediately recognizing the tall woman who came in with a small group of people. She looked elegant in a slim black suit that turned her red-gold hair to fire. For a moment, pride filled Everett, but it was quickly replaced by mingled sadness and regret.

Glancing down at the food he no longer wanted, he wished he could escape. To do so in the nearly empty room would draw unwanted attention to him, so he stayed where he was.

"Coffees all around?" asked a young man with the group. He wore a navy-blue suit and a tie, but Everett didn't recognize him.

"Tea for me, please," the woman, Leslie Logan, replied as another man held out her chair.

Everett was pleased that she sat where he could see her face. When she talked, she gestured gracefully with her hands. Once, she touched the pearls around her neck, making him wonder if they were a gift from her husband, Terrence. Everett liked the idea that he would give her presents to show his love.

The young man returned to the table with a tray of mugs. When he set down Leslie's tea, she smiled and thanked him. She always knew what to say and how to act. If things had been different, Everett, too, would have been raised to know exactly how to behave in every situation.

As if Leslie sensed his gaze on her, she looked right at him. When she smiled and waved, he thought his heart would stop. Did she somehow recognize him? He would have remembered her coming into his department.

He was halfway to his feet when he realized what he was doing. She was just being nice because she'd seen him gawking at her. Quickly he crouched down as though he had dropped something on the floor. When he straightened again, she had turned away, forgetting all about him.

Tears stung Everett's eyes as he stabbed his fork into the lukewarm lasagna and took a bite. It nearly made him gag, but he forced himself to chew and swallow. After he had blotted his mouth with a napkin, he pushed his tray to one side and picked up his book. He pretended to read it so that no one would think he sat alone because he had no friends.

The group of people talked and drank their coffee while he sat there turning pages. Other people came and went. An old man with glasses and thinning hair mopped the floor in the far corner with big slow circles.

After a few minutes Leslie laughed and the sound was like music. Everett closed his eyes and pretended she was laughing because he had said something to her that was really, really clever. When he opened his eyes again, her group was walking out the door. The man holding it open smiled down at her when she went past him.

Everett wished he could talk to Nancy about her, but he knew that wasn't possible. Nancy would never understand. The only one who might understand how he felt was Charlie, because he was Everett's friend.

Four

Morgan sat in the camp office, absently listening to the hoot of an owl. The first week of camp was nearly over and it had gone as smoothly as anything did involving nearly thirty children, many of whom were troubled.

The different groups came together to salute the flag each morning before breakfast. They took nature walks geared to their particular age group, made handprints out of clay, went rafting on the lake and performed original skits at the nightly campfire. They played tag, softball and soccer.

Jeff and Derrick had dealt with skinned knees, blisters, insect bites, scratches and a sprained wrist. Morgan had mediated a couple of quarrels and meted out extra chores for minor rule infractions.

His temporary office consisted of borrowed space in the lodge. It contained a scarred wood desk, two chairs, one of which wobbled on unsteady legs, and a file cabinet. Brief histories on each camper were kept in its one locking drawer.

Morgan did paperwork by lantern light. Someday, he thought, he'd probably go blind from the strain, but watching the changes taking place in his charges was easily worth the sacrifice. The smiles and sounds of laughter kept him coming back every year.

He sealed an envelope, stuck a stamp on the front and thought about calling his parents. After their recent visit to Portland, they'd gone home via Highway 101 down the Oregon coast.

He glanced at his watch, surprised at the time. His parents turned in early and rose with the dawn for an early walk, so maybe he'd call tomorrow instead.

Pushing back his chair, he stretched his arms overhead to ease the kinks. In the morning he was taking the older boys on a hike. If he was lucky, none of them would try sneaking a smoke. Summer forest fires were always a danger. Camp rules about contraband were strictly enforced, bags searched upon arrival and violators sent home early. Despite every precaution, the stuff still found its way in. Kids thought they could outwit the grown-ups.

Morgan got to his feet and bent from the waist, letting his arms hang limp. As the blood rushed to his head, he peered between his bare legs and saw two feet in sturdy shoes appear in the doorway.

"You busy?" asked a familiar female voice.

"Just hanging around," he quipped before straightening back up and turning around. His face felt hot.

"Ha ha," Emma said dryly, but at least she smiled.

"Come on in," he invited, tugging at the hem of his shirt.

He was pleased with the job she'd been doing. Not only did she appear to fit in easily with the other adults, but her warm manner seemed to endear her to many of the children, as well. She had brought up a few of her concerns during staff meetings, but this was the first time she had sought Morgan out alone.

"Am I interrupting?" She held up two mugs. "I brought you some decaf, black with one sugar."

She handed it to him as he pulled out a chair.

"I've just finished," he replied, flattered that she had noticed his preference. "Have a seat."

For a moment they studied each other silently as they blew on their steaming mugs. There was a line he didn't cross when it came to female co-workers, either here or at the agency, but the tug of attraction he felt toward Emma was persistent despite his attempts to ignore it.

He couldn't help but wonder what she was thinking.

"Have you gotten anywhere with Heather?" he

asked. The young teen's file indicated that a temporary placement had recently gone sour and she'd been sent back into foster care. Emma was concerned that she might be anorexic.

"She doesn't eat much," Emma replied. "I know it's the style to be thin, but she seems so withdrawn. Franny's keeping an eye on her, but I'm thinking about sending a report to Heather's caseworker when we get back. I'm not an expert, though. What do you think?"

"That would be appropriate," Morgan replied.

Despite her obvious concern, Emma's eyes glowed with enthusiasm when she talked about a couple of the other campers. "Emily and Petie seem to have bonded. Petie makes friends easily and she draws shy Emily along with her."

"I'm glad you came with us this year," Morgan blurted, trying not to stare at her soft lips. Realizing that she might take his remark personally, he quickly added, "You're great with the kids and you work hard."

"Thanks, boss," she replied, smiling widely as though they were sharing a joke. "Sounds like I can count on you for a good recommendation."

"Is that why you're here?" he asked, sipping his decaf. "It can't be merely for the generous salary and the employee benefits."

She set down her coffee with a considering expression. "It pays better than the video store where I was working and I thought it would be a terrific addition to my résumé," she reminded him after a moment.

Morgan ignored the whisper of disappointment. What had he expected her to say? And what would she do if he leaned forward and kissed that satiny mouth? If she didn't pull away, would it be because she liked him or because he was the boss and she had no choice?

"Any job leads?" he asked.

She shook her head with a rueful expression. "All the school districts seem to be facing budget constraints, but something will come up." Sitting back, she pushed at her hair with both hands. The motion emphasized the shape of her breasts in the gray Husky T-shirt.

He wanted to ask if she'd gone to the University of Washington, but figured it would make her aware of the direction of his gaze. Instead he dragged it back to her face.

He noticed a smile playing at the corners of her full mouth. Was she flirting? He would have to be more careful to hide his own attraction. After everything she had been through, she must feel vulnerable. He would never take advantage.

"I think it's really wonderful what you're doing here," she said. "It's nice to see someone taking the time to make a difference."

The part of him struggling to overcome his desire to

pull Emma into his arms ached for her to see him as a dynamic and desirable male rather than a kindly scout leader. "It's a group effort," he reminded her. "The Logans have been especially supportive."

"Well, it's great." Emma glanced at her watch and shot to her feet. "I'd better let you finish up," she said, her cheeks pink. "I didn't mean to keep you so long."

"I appreciate the decaf," he said, holding up his empty cup as he, too, stood up. "Was there something else you wanted to discuss?"

The play of the lantern light against her face cast a soft glow on her exquisite bone structure while the shadows turned her eyes to mysterious pools. He felt a jolt of regret that he must not act on his attraction, but he quickly brushed it aside. As long as they were here at the camp, his hands were tied. But afterward he might see whether she returned his interest.

"I'll see you in the morning," Emma replied, her warm smile restored as she reached out for his mug. "I'll wash these out."

"Thanks again," he replied as she turned away.

He listened as her footsteps grew fainter. Without her presence in the office, the light seemed to have dimmed and the air felt chillier.

Morgan scrubbed a hand over his face. He was getting fanciful, but tomorrow he would need his wits for the hike. The older boys were always a challenge, one that would surely take his mind off Emma.

* * *

As Emma supervised some of the younger boys who were seated at an outdoor table doing leather crafts, she kept thinking about Morgan. For the last few days she had made every excuse to seek him out. Franny and Sarah had begun to tease her, and she'd noticed Jeff elbow him last night as the campfire broke up and she approached Morgan with a question.

The other staff members were protective of their leader, but none of them suspected the real motive behind Emma's pursuit. The better she got to know Morgan, the more difficult it became to stick to her plan. Not only was he physically attractive, but he seemed to be a genuinely terrific guy. Too nice for what she had in mind, she thought with a sigh. Giving up wasn't an option, so what choice did she have but to proceed?

"Emma, am I doing this right?" asked a little boy named Carl, distracting her.

She looked down at the wallet he was making as a gift for his secret buddy at the end of the session. The two pieces of leather were laced up incorrectly. She should have been paying closer attention, but the mistake could be corrected.

"I think we need to undo this part," she said after she'd studied the wallet for a minute.

"I've ruined it!" he cried dramatically. "I knew I couldn't do it right."

The other boys looked on with interest as Carl

stamped his foot. His eyes filled with tears and his face flushed dark red.

Emma immediately squatted down so she was at eye level with the little boy. Carl and his younger brother had been split up a few months before when a couple opted to adopt only one of them. Even though Carl insisted that he understood why he had been left behind, he'd been acting out ever since. His foster parents were at their wits' end, hoping this break would be good for all three of them.

"The wallet's not ruined," Emma said softly as she pulled out the vinyl laces. "I'll show you what to do, okay? The stitches were nice and even. You're doing a good job, see?"

It was hard to keep herself from scooping him into a hug, but she didn't want to embarrass him further in front of the other boys. She contented herself with a grin and a wink.

In a few moments she had undone the stitching and shown him where he went wrong. As soon as he sat down with a gusty sigh and went back to work, she checked on the progress of the other wallets and key cases.

The sunny weather had been perfect all week, more comfortable than the muggy heat wave back in Portland. Ivy had complained about it when Emma had called last night to make sure her cat wasn't pining away. After lecturing Emma about not doing anything foolish, Ivy reassured her that Posy was fine.

As Emma sat at the table with the boys in her craft class, she tipped back her head and looked at the intensely blue sky through the tops of trees. The straight trunks of the Douglas firs seemed to go up for miles.

"Look," she said to Carl as she pointed. "I'll bet that's a hawk perched on that dead spar tree."

"Yesterday we saw a pair of bald eagles," he told her excitedly. "Jeff took us on a nature walk around the lake. He said eagles were endangered, but they're coming back and that you can always recognize them by their white heads."

"We saw some deer tracks, too," added one of the other boys.

"And rabbit poop!" shouted a third, which of course sent them all into paroxysms of laughter and made Emma smile.

"Did you see any wildflowers?" she asked with an innocent expression.

"Flowers! No way!" two of them exclaimed in unison.

For a few minutes Emma asked them more about the various birds, animals and plants they had seen. The sun warmed her bare arms as an intermittent breeze blew through the dry trees.

The sound of Morgan's voice in the distance alerted Emma that he was back from town. She ignored the flutter of anticipation she felt.

A little while later, he appeared on the path from the lodge wearing sunglasses and a baseball cap.

"How's Mohammed?" Emma called out.

At the sound of her voice, Morgan changed direction. Perhaps it was her imagination, but his expression behind the tinted lenses seemed to brighten as he came over to the table.

"Mo needed a few stitches, but he'll be fine," Morgan said, removing his shades as he glanced at the boys with her. "I suppose everyone heard what happened."

"It was the hot topic at breakfast," Emma replied. "Derrick said he sliced open his hand while he was helping Cookie. Derrick bandaged the cut, but he thought it needed stitches."

"Did he bleed in the food?" Carl asked.

"Only yours," Emma told him, laughing.

"We wanted to make sure that Mo hadn't damaged any tendons," Morgan explained. "I drove him to the walk-in clinic in Sisters. It's about fifteen miles from here."

Some of the others had talked about the town one night at the campfire. Emma remembered someone saying that it had a quaint western ambience.

"Did they use regular thread to sew him up?" asked one of the boys she was helping.

"That's gross!" exclaimed another. "Do you think he'll let us see it?"

"I guess you'll have to ask Mo about all that later," Morgan replied, folding his arms across his wide chest. "He came back with me, but right now he's resting."

Morgan wore baggy gray shorts and a royal-blue

polo shirt that matched his eyes. His muscular legs had the same golden tan as his face and arms.

After seeing him dressed this way for more than a week, it was getting more difficult for Emma to conjure up the image from her first meeting with his alter ego in the suit and tie.

Her frustration at that meeting was much easier for her to recall. When she thought about him, which seemed to be most of the time, that frustration was what she needed to remember—not how great he looked.

While the boys continued to hash over the idea of getting their skin pierced with a sewing needle, Morgan switched his attention to Emma.

"There's something I need to discuss with you," he said, flashing his white teeth. "Think you could leave these ruffians alone for a minute?"

Her heart began to thump as she got up from the table. "Sure, I g-guess so," she stammered.

Her physical attraction to him was as unwanted as it was unexpected. She had to stay focused. With a slight feeling of trepidation, she followed him as he put several feet between them and the table.

"Is there a problem?" she asked, glancing down at the ground, covered with dry needles. "Something I've done wrong?"

"What? Oh, no, not at all. You've been doing a terrific job." Morgan must have seen the concern on her face, because he gave her shoulder a quick squeeze. "Especially for a city slicker," he added teasingly.

His words eased away her sudden tension and her shoulder tingled pleasantly from his touch.

"I'm glad to hear that." She laced the fingers of both hands together. "What's on your mind?"

"I need a favor," he said gravely.

Something sparked inside her. She had to swallow the word *anything* before it could pop out of her mouth.

"What's that?" she asked, cheeks flushing.

"You work so hard as it is," he continued, apparently oblivious to her stumbling response. "If we shuffle your duties around, could you fill in for Mo? It's just for a couple of days until another volunteer can get here."

"You want me to sleep with the boys in Falcon?" she asked, using the group name they had chosen. Mohammed's group was in their early teens and she had noticed a couple of them ogling her when they thought she wasn't looking.

Morgan looked startled. "No, no. I wouldn't ask that of you. Mo will continue to supervise Falcon, but he's not supposed to get his hand wet, so he can't help Cookie. I know you're doing a lot of the KP already, but Sarah and Franny are working with the girls on the final skit, or I'd ask them."

Emma's flush deepened. She'd been so busy gawking at Morgan like a girl with a crush that she had leaped ahead. "I get along great with Cookie. Of course I'll be happy to do whatever I can."

"Great, thanks. Cookie's got lunch under control, but he'll talk to you about supper, okay?" Morgan backed away. "I've got a lot to do, so I'll see you later."

After two days of helping out with meals as well as fulfilling her counselor duties, not only was Emma bone-deep exhausted, but she'd had no time to further her relationship with Morgan. Who would have had any idea that preparing camp food would take up so much time?

Not her.

Even with everyone else pitching in when they could, Cookie worked darned hard. He insisted on making everything from scratch, serving well-balanced and nutritious meals. For dinner tonight they'd had a green salad, baked chicken, seasoned rice, peas and sourdough biscuits.

While he was in the dining room serving the brownies he'd baked for dessert, Emma had been putting away the last of the clean pots and pans Heidi had washed. As Emma wiped off the counter for the last time, she started thinking about the countless family meals and holiday dinners she had shared with the people she'd thought were her parents.

Her mother was a wonderful cook who loved to entertain. She had teased Emma on more than one occasion about her lack of interest in cooking. Emma knew the basics, but she had never shared Sally Wright's passion for reading cookbooks and clipping new recipes from magazines.

Memories flooded over Emma as she rinsed out the cloth she had used on the counters. Convulsively she clenched it in her fist as she stood at the sink with her head bowed.

Guess you really knew all along why I didn't share your talent in the kitchen, Mom, she thought, squeezing her eyes shut to keep the tears from leaking out.

The Wrights didn't even know she was here. They still left phone messages for her at the apartment, but she never returned their calls. Of course that didn't mean she didn't miss them. Beneath her hurt and anger, she still loved them both.

Otherwise knowing the truth wouldn't have been so hard.

She understood now why people spent their entire lives searching for their biological parents, or looking for the baby they had once chosen to give up. It might appear selfish or intrusive, but Emma got it, she really did.

Her own situation hadn't been getting any easier to accept as time passed. It grew more difficult, her need to know more desperate.

She was unable to move forward, to go on with her life until she knew what lay behind her. What were the circumstances of her birth and why, why, *why* had she been placed for adoption at all?

Hearing a noise behind her, she pinned a smile on her

face, blinked away any telltale tears and turned around, expecting to see Cookie in the doorway. Instead Morgan stood there with a plate in his hand.

"I saved you a brownie."

He knew that seeking her out was probably a mistake. They had gotten in the habit of exchanging a few words after the campfire was over, or when she stopped by his office as he did paperwork. He hadn't realized how much he looked forward to seeing her until tonight when she hadn't shown up. He should have let it go.

"You look beat," he said bluntly.

She was standing by the counter with a dishrag in one hand, her hair waving wildly. Her eyes looked huge in her pale face, and whatever color she normally slicked over her mouth had long since worn off.

A hard jolt went through Morgan, leaving him shaken. He shouldn't be tempting himself like this.

She looked at the plate in his hand. He was amazed to see that it wasn't shaking.

"I'll split it with you," Emma said. "Would you like something to drink?"

Struggling for normality, he glanced at the six-burner monstrosity that was fueled with propane.

"Whatever you're having would be fine," he managed.

"Tea it is." While she busied herself with the fixings, he nearly fell into one of the chairs at the small table by the wall.

What was his problem? He'd run the camp program year after year, surrounded by women staffers, and never felt more than friendship and passing attraction.

With Emma, his spirits lifted whenever he saw her. Realizing that he needed to corral his interest, what had he done? He'd sought her out instead.

"Can I do anything to help?" he asked.

"Nope." She set down their mugs of tea and the brownie that she had cut in two. "I hope you don't mind." She added a pair of candles. "No point in wasting propane."

She turned off the lanterns, leaving the rest of the kitchen in shadows. Before Morgan could get to his feet, she'd plopped herself in the chair opposite him, apparently oblivious to the sense of intimacy the candlelight created.

"What a day," she said, spooning sugar into her tea. "How about you?"

He was amazed by the ease he felt, as though ending their day together had become a comfortable routine despite the awareness between them.

This was what a relationship should be, he thought suddenly. It took an effort for Morgan to drag himself away from places he had no business being.

As she sipped her tea, Emma watched him over the brim of her mug.

"Heavy thoughts?" she prodded, breaking the silence between them.

"Just the usual." He fiddled with his teabag. "Reviewing tomorrow's schedule in my head."

She nodded without speaking.

"You're a good listener," he realized aloud. "Without meaning to sound sexist because I'm really not referring only to women, I have to say that's a rare commodity. So many people are only at ease with noise."

"Thank you, I think."

Her answering smile drew his attention back to her full lips. Unwelcome awareness shot through him.

He glanced out the window. Except for their small circle of light, the rest of the camp was dark and quiet. After lights-out, flashlights were allowed only for nocturnal trips to the privy.

"I think this is my favorite time of the day," he admitted as he stared down at his tea.

"Why is that?" Emma broke off a piece of the divided brownie and ate it.

A good listener could draw out secrets that a person never meant to reveal, as could a few well-chosen questions. Morgan had used that strategy himself, both at work and in his personal life. He weighed each word carefully.

"Every day's a challenge. By nightfall, I know how well it's been met."

"Why do you do all this?" She made a sweeping gesture with her hand. "Don't get me wrong. Bringing these kids here every year is a fabulous thing to do, but it's got to be a huge commitment of your time and effort.

Do you ever think about quitting and letting someone else take over?"

He leaned forward. "You're good," he said appreciatively. "I can't imagine why your school district let you go."

She straightened away from him, looking offended. "I don't know what you mean."

"It was a compliment, Emma. You have the gift of making someone feel important. You make me want to tell you things I don't normally share." He stirred his cooling tea. "I've watched you with the kids here at camp. They open up to you. With some of them, it's not easy to gain their trust, but you seem to manage."

"I'm only doing my job," she murmured.

"And I'll write you a great recommendation," he replied. "I'm sure you'll find something soon."

She sighed and pushed the brownie plate toward him. "Thank you."

"How are things with your family?" he asked carefully.

Her rueful smile faded, her gaze turning blank. "Nothing's changed. I'm still adopted and they still kept it from me."

"Have you tried talking to them again?" he persisted.

She shook her head, staring down at her hands.

He ignored the urge to push back his chair and get to his feet, to pull her up with him and wrap her in his arms. The desire to offer comfort was tangled with the craving to feel her body pressed tightly against him.

"I'm sure they love you," he stammered.

She lifted her chin and looked at him. "I'm not sure of anything. You don't know what it's like."

Beneath the anger in her voice he could hear the hurt.

"Every person's situation is different," he said carefully. "I wouldn't presume to know exactly how you feel, but I have some idea."

"Because you work at Children's Connection?" she sneered.

Giving in to his need to touch her, he reached across the table and covered her hand with his. Her skin felt cold to the touch. He wasn't surprised when she pulled away.

"No, Emma," he said quietly. "Not because of my job. Because I'm adopted, too."

Five

Morgan's announcement caught Emma by surprise, but it certainly explained a lot about his involvement with the camp as well as the agency.

"Were you a baby when you were adopted?" she asked, assuming that he would never have brought up the subject unless he was willing to discuss it.

"No, I was three years old." He took a sip of the tea and then he set the mug back down.

"Do you want to go for a walk?" he asked abruptly, shoving back his chair without waiting for her answer. "The moon's pretty bright, but I've got a flashlight, just in case."

Emma couldn't ignore the opportunity to spend more

time with him. Besides, she was too curious to refuse. "Sure. A little fresh air would probably help me sleep."

He rinsed out the mugs while she wiped off the table and put away the sugar. Everything was kept tightly sealed so as not to attract ants.

She leaned across the table to blow out the candles, and they used the flashlight until they got outside.

"Give your eyes a chance to adjust," he suggested as they stood on the porch.

After a moment, during which neither of them spoke, they headed together toward the lake. At one point he took her hand in order to lead her around some rocks, his grip warm and reassuring. To her disappointment he dropped it again almost immediately, leaving her struggling with her reaction to his touch.

As she followed him silently along the path, the moonlight illuminated the shape of his head and his broad shoulders. Ignoring her sharp awareness of Morgan as a man wasn't easy. She wanted to ask why he was still single, but that might alert him to her interest. Her curiosity would have to wait.

The raft and a few rowboats were secured to a short wooden dock next to the roped-off swimming area. They bobbed around, the movement making occasional soft noises. Farther along the shoreline, the water was thick with lily pads and fat brown cattails with their swordlike leaves. They weren't visible now, but she had noticed them the first day she'd come down here.

"The stars are breathtaking," she said after she and Morgan stopped at the lakeshore. "It's true what people say about being able to see them so much better once you get away from city lights."

Morgan had stopped by a wooden bench that faced the small lake. "And people who look at the sky while they're walking can end up getting wet," he teased as they sat on the bench with a foot of space between them. "But you're right about the stars. They always make me feel pretty insignificant."

There was no breeze, so the moon's reflection across the surface of the lake was like liquid silver on black velvet. The spicy scent of the fir needles seemed stronger out here, too.

Emma was beginning to understand what drew people to the outdoors. There was a lot more to it than RVs, ATVs and noisy beer drinkers sitting around a fire pit swapping stories.

Tucking one leg under her, she turned toward Morgan. "You must have been an adorable baby with your dark hair and blue eyes. Why weren't you adopted until you were three?"

"How do you know I was adorable?" In the moonlight, his expression was teasing, his dimple a dark smudge against his cheek.

She saw the trap his question laid, but walked right in. "Because you're a very attractive adult."

For the space of a couple of heartbeats, he didn't respond. She wondered if she'd embarrassed him.

"Are you always so outspoken?" he finally asked, his voice sounding unusually strained.

She thought of the role she'd been playing since she had arrived here, pushing him as much as she dared without being too obvious about her intentions.

"Sometimes, I guess," she hedged, steering the conversation back to him. "I hope I didn't make you uncomfortable."

"I'm flattered that a beautiful woman finds me attractive." He glanced away as an owl hooted from the woods.

"So, where are your parents?" she asked before the silence could become uncomfortable.

He turned his attention back to Emma. "They're enjoying retirement down in California, where I grew up. In fact, they were up here visiting me just recently."

It took her a moment to catch on. "Oh, you must be talking about the people who raised you."

"Those *are* my parents," he said firmly. "I'm lucky to have them." Then he blew out a breath. "But I know what you're asking. My birth mother came from Mexico. She was looking for a better life, but instead she had a brief affair and ended up with me."

That explained the golden tan and jet-black hair.

"The only thing I know about my biological father is that he was a blue-eyed Caucasian," Morgan added. "It was enough."

Emma would have liked to pat Morgan's arm. She didn't want him to misinterpret the gesture, so she kept her hands clasped together tightly in her lap while she tried to absorb what he'd said.

"So your mother tried to raise you alone?" she guessed, trying to imagine how terribly difficult it would be to find yourself alone in a strange country with a baby.

He nodded. "It must not have been easy for her," he said as though he were reading Emma's thoughts, "but eventually she ended up cleaning my father's offices. He told me that one day she asked him if he knew a nice couple who would take me. She wanted to go back home, but she wanted me to have a better life. It was a private adoption, but a legal one."

"They paid her?" Emma asked, trying to make out his expression.

"Only enough for her to go back to her village and start over. She refused to accept any more than that."

A wave of envy washed over Emma—envy at the knowledge he possessed about his own birth mother and that he withheld from Emma about hers.

She swallowed hard. "And you've been in contact with her since then?"

He surprised her by shaking his head. "No, not at all."

When he didn't add anything more, she peered up at his face. "How could you not be curious? She's your mother."

"She gave birth to me," he corrected her gently. "I

wish her well for giving me a chance, but I don't need anything from her. I have a family."

He reached up to touch Emma's face lightly with his fingertips. "You have your parents, too, and I'm sure they care about you very deeply." His voice was deep and soft. "Have you thought about calling them?"

As she considered how to answer his question, she forced herself to break the enticing contact before she made a fool of herself.

"I haven't decided yet what to do." It was the truth, more or less.

She wasn't about to admit how much time she'd spent imagining a fantasy reunion with her birth parents. They would be delighted to see her again, their eyes sparkling with tears and their faces alight with pride. What if they truly did regret their decision to give her up. Unless she was able to find them and ask if they'd had second thoughts, they would never know she cared.

For a few moments neither she nor Morgan said anything. In the lake a fish jumped with a splash. Ever-widening rings spread across the water, marring its smooth surface.

Emma hated to spoil the peace of the moment by suggesting they go back to the lodge, but the hour had to be growing late.

"The stars are even more breathtaking from some of the alpine meadows," Morgan said quietly. "As corny as it sounds, from the higher elevations it really does seem as though you could reach up and pick them, like fairy lights."

"Are there any of those meadows around here?" she asked innocently. Heidi had already mentioned how Morgan always took a day before the session was over for a long solo hike. This time Emma was determined to accompany him.

"There are several meadows in the general area," he replied warily.

"We should take the kids on a hike to one of them." She let eagerness fill her voice. "Wouldn't there be wild-flowers? The girls would enjoy them, even if the boys didn't."

His face was once again in profile. "The closest meadow is nearly a three-hour hike. There's a lake and a shelter for hikers who want to spend the night, but no other facilities, if you get my meaning."

He turned toward her. "Thirty kids asking 'where's the rest room?' isn't my idea of fun."

"Maybe you and I could hike up there," she suggested daringly. "I'd love to see it before I have to go back."

Morgan seemed to freeze. "You mean just the two of us?"

She chuckled softly. "We could take a chaperone along, if you think we'd need one."

Damn, but she shouldn't have said that. If she acted flirtatiously, she would spook him for sure.

"I don't think it's a good idea." His voice had gone flat.

She tried to swallow her disappointment. "Taking a chaperone?"

"It's not that I don't enjoy your company," he continued, ignoring her comment, "but I wouldn't want to start any gossip about either of us."

"The session will be over in a few days," she argued. "What other people might think is no big deal."

"You might not be coming back next year," he said firmly, "but I am. As a leader, I have a reputation to maintain and an example to set. Even the appearance of impropriety needs to be avoided, especially around kids."

His adamant tone left Emma speechless.

With his head bent, Morgan pinched the bridge of his nose. "My God, that sounds so damned pompous," he muttered, half to himself. "It's just that I was raised to live my life by a certain standard, that's all."

"I understand what you're saying," she replied, ecstatic that he hadn't flat-out refused.

She pushed aside the twinge of guilt. If he ended up compromising his principles, it would be his choice. No one was going to hold a gun to his head, after all.

"It's just that I've never been camping before. When I was growing up, the Wrights weren't big on roughing it." The three of them had taken several fun vacations to theme parks and other tourist meccas. "Until I came here, I had no idea what I was missing," she added. "Just being here has opened up a whole new world for me."

She glanced down at her hands, sighing deeply. "I

hate to think about going back to Portland without seeing as much of this beautiful area as I possibly can, that's all. Who knows where I'll end up working next. I may have to relocate and not have the chance to come back."

"I hadn't realized your feelings about camping had changed so much," Morgan said thoughtfully. "I'm glad you've developed a deeper appreciation."

"If you let me go on the hike with you, I won't slow you down," she promised rashly. "I've got enough stamina for a three-hour hike."

"It's three hours up and three more back down," he reminded her.

"I can do it."

"I was planning to go up to Johnson Lake on Sunday. Actually the terrain isn't that difficult." He seemed to be measuring each word. "Let me think about it, okay?"

"Sure, that would be great." Instinct told her to back off for now. "I guess we'd better go in," she said with genuine regret. "It's getting pretty late, but I want to thank you for taking the time to talk to me. It helps me to hear a different viewpoint about being adopted."

It had been a shock to find out about Morgan's background, but she couldn't help but feel some resentment, too. Just because he had no interest in his birth mother didn't give him the right to make decisions for someone else—someone whose feelings were vastly different from his.

* * *

Everett walked through the main lobby of Children's Connection, but he didn't see anyone who interested him. With the director gone on vacation for two weeks, Leslie Logan and some of the other major donors hadn't been around. He had overheard someone say that the Logans were visiting friends in the San Juan Islands of Washington State.

As Everett stopped to look out the glass front doors, he wondered what it would be like to have the money to travel, like the Logans did. They could afford whatever they wanted.

He wasn't greedy, but who could blame him for wanting a few extra bucks to spend on nice things? He'd like to impress Nancy with a fancy present or a fabulous cruise. He would hand her his gold card and tell her to buy whatever she wanted. Or he would pick out some jewelry, like celebrities were always doing, and surprise her with it. She would be so happy that she would smile at him as though he was really somebody.

"Everett. Everett!"

He blinked, realizing that someone was speaking to him. When he turned, one of the other accountants was giving him a disgusted look.

"Jeez, were you in some kind of trance?" demanded Bob Roach, hands thrust into the pockets of his fancy slacks.

Unlike Everett, Bob was one of those people who

seemed to have been born knowing the rules: how to dress, what to say and how to act. Everett overheard him talking all the time about the parties he threw at his condo. He was always organizing a group to stop at one of the local pubs after work. Sometimes he asked Everett to finish up a project for him so he could leave early, because he had "big plans."

"Uh, yeah, Bob." Everett tried to keep the eagerness from his voice as he pushed back his hair. He knew he'd failed when the other man's lip curled into a sneer.

"I'm taking a long lunch, if you know what I mean," Bob said with a wink. "If anyone asks, I had a doctor appointment, okay?"

"Sure, Bob," Everett replied, even though he *wasn't* sure what Bob meant. They all got an hour for lunch. Wasn't that long enough? "You can count on me," he added.

"That's my buddy," Bob called over his shoulder.

As Bob began to whistle, Everett smiled widely at his retreating back. Wait until Everett got the extra money he was expecting. He'd be able to afford some cool clothes, like Bob wore. Instead of going to the bar where Everett stopped every night to eat dinner alone, he would go out with Bob and his friends.

Maybe Everett would invite them over to the new place he was going to have one day soon, but only if they were nice to him. Like Bob and Nancy.

* * *

As hard as he tried, Morgan wasn't able to concentrate on the packet of office mail spread before him on his desk. Jeff had brought it back with him from the post office in Sisters this morning, along with the fresh produce for the rest of the week.

Morgan's thoughts kept straying back to Emma and their conversation down by the lake the night before. He didn't consider himself to be especially vain, but he could usually tell when a woman was interested.

While they were here, she was off-limits, he reminded himself with a sigh of disappointment. His father had taught him about ethical conduct. There were some things a person just didn't do. Getting involved with a co-worker, especially a subordinate, was one of them. Having a personal relationship with a client was another. The camp session might be temporary, but Emma's connection to the agency where Morgan worked was not.

He was relieved that she seemed to have given up on her quest for information about her birth parents. There was no reason for her to ever know that she was the product of a brief affair between a married senator and his intern. The man would never jeopardize his political career or his marriage by acknowledging the baby he'd fathered out of wedlock. Nor would the intern, who had been handsomely paid for her silence, and who still worked in D.C.

Morgan wished he could ask his father's advice about

taking Emma with him tomorrow, but he knew what the doctor would say. *The appearance of impropriety is no less damaging to one's reputation than the act of impropriety itself.*

Morgan would never do anything to jeopardize the agency's reputation, but neither would he want to discourage someone's budding interest in nature and the outdoors. Propping both elbows on his desk, he rested his chin in his hands and stared out the window. For a man used to making decisions, he was certainly waffling on this one!

During her free period, Emma sat at a table on the back porch of the lodge and finished writing her comments about the girl she had originally thought might have an eating disorder. To Emma's relief, Heather's appetite appeared to be fine, nor had Emma seen her sneak off by herself after meals.

Heather had made a couple of friends in her cabin, called Hip Hop, and she participated in the activities. Maybe she was just naturally thin, but Emma didn't have the training to evaluate her further.

Heather's file was the last one that needed updating. When Emma was finished, she closed the folder with a sigh of relief. She missed her computer, but she had a little while to enjoy the solitude before it was time to assist Sarah's girls with a jewelry-making project.

Emma stared at the line of raw mountain peaks jutting above the trees. They reminded her of boulders that had been set in place by giant hands. There were still a couple of patches of dirty snow at the highest elevations.

The days were flying by. Before she knew it, the session would be over and with it her last opportunity to influence Morgan. She had to persuade him to take her with him tomorrow.

At breakfast this morning he had seemed distant. She'd overheard him saying that he and Derrick, who was a certified lifeguard, were going to take the little boys out in the boats for a picnic lunch on the far shore. They would be gone until late in the afternoon.

During her free period, Emma welcomed the break from keeping a constant smile plastered on her face. Was twenty-seven too old to be homesick? She missed Posy, and she missed her friends. What few she had left.

In truth, Emma also missed the Wrights, although she would never admit it. She wondered whether they were still leaving messages on her machine or if they had finally given up.

Had they said anything to Emma's aunt and uncle in Spokane? Her cousins in Boise and Medford? What did any of them think, or had everyone on both sides of the family always known about Emma's adoption? Had no one felt that she had a right to be told?

She was sitting with her feet propped on the porch rail and her eyes closed when she heard footsteps behind her. Perhaps one of the other women had a break, too.

"So this is where you hide when you want to goof off."

Morgan walked around in front of her as she put her feet down. His cheeks were flushed below the brim of his Mariner's cap, and a rivulet of perspiration trickled down the side of his neck. Since their arrival over a week before, his tanned arms and legs had deepened to bronze.

"Warm out?" she asked. Her chair was in the shade.

Removing his cap, he wiped his forehead with one muscular forearm.

"The lake's nice, but rowing back was hot work."

"Maybe you should have jumped in," she suggested teasingly.

The memory of seeing him in swim trunks during the inner-tube races, his body surprisingly athletic, made her mouth go dry.

He didn't return her smile. "We'll leave after breakfast tomorrow for Johnson Lake," he said. "Plan on being gone most of the day."

As soon as the meaning behind his words sank in, Emma leaped to her feet. "Oh, thank you!"

He took a step back, his expression wary and his arm extended, palm out, as though to ward her off. "No problem."

She would have liked to ask why he'd changed his mind, but he didn't give her the chance. After she watched him walk away, she made a list of the few things she needed in her day pack.

The rest of the day seemed to drag, despite her kitchen duties and craft classes. That evening after the campfire with its usual skits and songs, she left Morgan alone. She was afraid of saying something that might change his mind.

"How did you talk our fearless leader into taking you with him tomorrow?" Sarah demanded when she caught up with Emma on the path back to the cabins. "That's like a pilgrimage for him or something. He always goes alone."

"Not always," Emma replied. "I told him I've never seen an Alpine meadow before, so he wanted to show me one."

Emma suspected Franny of having a secret crush on Morgan, but Sarah had a boyfriend back in Woodburn. She talked about him all the time, making no secret of how much she missed him. He was supposed to have come to camp with Sarah, but apparently he couldn't get the time off from his job at the outlet mall. He worked there during summer break from OSU, where the two of them were students.

"I think Morgan likes you," Sarah whispered. "As far as I know, he's never taken anyone else with him. The wildflowers are probably an excuse, like showing you his etchings or something."

Emma ignored the sudden jump in her pulse. "I think you're wrong. We're just friends. Once the camp session is over, we'll go our separate ways."

Sarah laughed knowingly. "I understand perfectly," she said with a wink.

Emma didn't bother to argue, but it took her a long

time to fall asleep that night. It seemed that as soon as she finally drifted off, reveille sounded.

She didn't see Morgan at breakfast. From across the table, Derrick handed her a note with her name scrawled across the outside.

"From the boss," he said, and her heart plunged down to her toes.

The staffers who weren't assigned to meals with the children all stared as Emma unfolded the piece of paper and silently read the bold handwriting.

Hike delayed until afternoon. Giving grand tour to potential patron this a.m.

Figuring the news would get around soon enough, she recited the contents aloud.

"That must be the owner of the fancy SUV in the parking lot," Heidi exclaimed. "Whoever they are, I hope they write a big fat check."

Everyone laughed and then they resumed eating. Emma moved her scrambled eggs around on her plate while she willed her stomach to calm down. Waiting several more hours wasn't going to be easy, but at least he hadn't canceled on her altogether.

Morgan set a steady pace that Emma had no trouble maintaining as she followed him through the trees that afternoon. The silence around them was calming; even their footsteps were muffled by the bed of needles that cushioned the path.

"You could be a professional guide," she said after he had pointed out a maidenhair fern with a thin black stem that looked like wire and frothy green leaves. "Is there anything you don't know about this area?"

"I'm far from an expert," he replied, stopping to take a swig from his water bottle. He tipped back his head, his throat muscles rippling as he swallowed.

Emma could have watched him all day, but instead she tore her gaze away before he noticed her gawking like a groupie.

"What's that?" she asked, spotting a small white flower sticking up from the needles. Its nearly translucent petals looked as though they had been carved from wax. "Is it real?"

"That's Indian pipe." He squatted down by the odd little specimen that grew next to a fallen log. His thigh muscles bulged. "Also called ice plant, ghost plant. Its official name is *Monotropa uniflora*."

"See what I mean?" she said with a laugh as she, too, bent down for a closer look. "I'm impressed, Mr. Davis. You're a walking encyclopedia."

The odd little plant was pure white, but a few nearby stalks had shriveled and turned black.

"Blame it on five years of dealing with kids and their inquisitive minds," Morgan drawled as he straightened back up and adjusted his pack. "Ready to move on?"

As they walked, their footsteps were nearly silent. The bright sunlight was filtered by the canopy of tree-tops far overhead, making the temperature pleasantly cool. The trunks of the fir trees were remarkably straight, the bark gray and rough.

Green moss, some of it as shaggy as a feather boa, covered the northern sides of the trees and scattered boulders. Growing through the moss was a type of fungus that looked like shelves, some gray and a smaller kind in a vibrant shade of orange.

Several varieties of ferns were scattered around in clumps, as were Oregon grape bushes with their inedible berries. Various sizes and shapes of toadstools sprouted around the fallen, rotting logs.

Eventually the trees began to thin out and the light was brighter. Sparse patches of grass appeared and the air became warmer.

Taking several breaks, they walked at an easy pace for nearly three hours. Most of it was up a gradual but steady incline. Ahead of them, the path curved around the base of a huge cedar tree and then disappeared over the next rise.

"Are you doing okay?" Morgan asked after he'd stopped to drink some water.

"I'm fine." Emma wouldn't have complained if her feet were falling off, but she hoped their destination was near. Her pack was getting heavy and she had been too excited to eat much lunch. Her stomach was starting to growl.

The trail widened, allowing them to walk side by side as they approached a small structure. Its sharply slanted roof was covered with moss and fir needles, its wood siding weathered to a pewter color.

"Here's the Hilton," Morgan quipped as they walked by. "Not that we'll be spending the night."

Emma hardly glanced at the building.

"Oh," she gasped softly as she cleared the top of the hill. Spread out before them was the meadow he had told her about. It was carpeted with grass and wildflowers. At the center of the clearing was a small sapphire-blue body of water.

"That's Johnson Lake," Morgan said as he stood beside her. "Pretty, isn't it?"

The lake and meadow were surrounded by tree-covered mountains. Towering in the distance was a row of bare, jagged peaks that appeared to be hewn from solid granite.

"I had no idea what it would feel like to be so close to the Cascade Range." Emma was totally sincere. "It takes my breath away."

Her reaction to the wild beauty was everything Morgan had hoped it might be. The sight moved him every time he came here.

"You aren't disappointed?" he probed.

She looked up at him with an expression of amazement. "Are you kidding? I was bowled over by the scenery on the drive up to camp, but this is truly incredible."

She surprised him by grabbing his hand. "Thank you so much for bringing me with you."

As he studied her upturned face, glowing with enthusiasm, sparkling with life, he couldn't remember when he had ever seen anything so lovely. He swayed closer, but the instant he realized what he was about to do, he jerked back, his cheeks flaming.

"Let's eat." He wondered if she had noticed his impulsive movement. "I'm starving."

When he had the nerve to glance her way again, he could see that her face had turned pink as she gazed at their surroundings. He had probably embarrassed her.

"Where's the best place to sit?" she asked brightly without meeting his gaze.

He didn't want her experience to be tainted by concern over what he might have in mind by bringing her here. He had to clear the air.

"Emma," he said softly as she turned in a wide circle with her arms flung out like Julie Andrews in *The Sound of Music*. "I'm sorry."

Emma whipped her head around as the sunlight shimmered in the waves of her hair. "Don't be." She came right up to him, so their bodies were nearly touching.

"Aren't you attracted to me?" she asked.

Morgan didn't consider himself a green kid who got easily tongue-tied when a woman hit on him. Despite a fair amount of experience in the singles scene, he was still surprised by Emma's bold question.

"My feelings don't matter," he finally croaked. "Acting on them would be inappropriate."

His answer must have pleased her, because her full lips curved into a smile. In response, his own awareness ratcheted up a couple hundred notches. Just what he needed while they were alone in the wilderness.

"I'll take that as a yes," she drawled, giving him a wink.

While he was still trying to come up with a neutral comment to diffuse the shimmering attraction between them, she slipped off her pack.

"Relax, Morgan," she said teasingly as she strutted away, her hips swinging. "I'm not going to jump you."

His reaction had been everything she'd hoped for, Emma reminded herself silently as they sat on the grass near the lake a little while later. Since the original plan had been to start out this morning, Cookie had packed them a sack lunch: sandwiches, chips, carrot sticks and peanut butter cookies for dessert, all spread out on the nylon jacket that had been rolled up in Morgan's backpack. While they demolished the food with enthusiasm, they discussed the progress that some of their charges were making.

"Being chosen to come here must help a little, after getting passed over or rejected by prospective parents," Emma commented between bites of her ham and cheese sandwich.

"It often seems to," Morgan replied. "God knows

that so many of these kids need something in their lives to make them feel special."

"Is that where you got the idea originally?" she asked curiously.

Mouth full, he nodded. "Some of them really tugged at my heart," he said after he'd swallowed. "Since we first began the project, it keeps growing. Although we've got some truly generous patrons, we have to turn kids away every year."

Emma finished the last of her sandwich as she watched a family of ducks swimming on the lake. "How did your meeting go this morning?"

The dimple flashed in Morgan's cheek. "He promised that he'd talk to his accountant and give me a call in a couple of weeks."

She held up her crossed fingers. "Good luck."

Six

For a long moment, Morgan battled the impulse to lean over and kiss Emma's cheek. Not only would the gesture be totally inappropriate, but he didn't trust himself to get that close and still be able to back away. Finally he raised his water bottle in a toast.

"Here's to good company," he said.

Emma's smile softened. "Thank you for bringing me with you."

He stretched out in the grass, chin propped on his arm so he could look at her. The only sounds were the distant quacking of the ducks paddling on the lake and the sigh of the breeze as it drifted through the nearby treetops.

"Whenever I begin to feel burned out at work, this

reminds me of my insignificance in the global scheme of things," he said.

"This sure beats my usual way of relaxing," she replied with a sigh.

"What would that be?" he asked.

"I like to read, but lately I've been bringing home a lot of old movies from the video store where I work."

He pictured her alone in a robe and fuzzy slippers, with a bowl of popcorn on her lap and the cat at her side. "What do you watch?"

"Anything with a good story," she said. "I'm not particular as long as it isn't too gory. How about you? Are you a movie buff?"

"Like you, as long as the plot makes sense, I'm not particular." He thought for a moment. "I do lean toward comedies over violence." For a few more moments they discussed their favorite actors and the movies they liked.

Using her pack as a pillow, Emma lay on her back and stared up at the sky. "Oh, look," she exclaimed, pointing upward. "Is that another bald eagle?"

Morgan rolled over and shaded his eyes with his hand. "I can't tell for sure, but it looks like one with that wingspan."

As she lay next to him, he wished that she was closer, with her head resting on his shoulder. He could almost feel her breasts pressing against his side.

His body reacted sharply, insistently. He turned his

head, afraid she might have noticed, but her eyes were closed.

Watching her chest rise and fall wasn't helping, so he studied the few clouds instead.

After a while she stirred and then sat up. After she had fluffed up her hair, she wrapped her arms around her bent knees.

He turned to his side so that he could see her. "What are you thinking?" he asked, feeling lazy.

Usually he came up here alone to spend some time gazing at the lake and the mountains. With Emma along, the experience was totally different. He wanted to call her once they got back to Portland. If it led to anything, he would just have to figure out a way to square his conscience with her connection to the clinic.

She stretched her arms over her head. "I can't get my mind off those peanut butter cookies in your pack," she admitted with a laugh.

"Got a sweet tooth?" he teased after he'd dug out the plastic bag and unzipped it.

"Chocolate doesn't tempt me, but I'm nuts about peanut butter," she replied, reaching for one. "It's like an Achilles' heel for me."

After she took the cookie, he held up an apple. "We've got two of these. Shall we save them for later?"

"Aren't I supposed to offer you the apple?" she teased, her voice a little husky as she looked into his eyes.

Awareness arced between them. Morgan was torn between his policy of keeping his distance and the desire to take her into his arms and flick the cookie crumbs from her lips with his tongue.

How badly he wanted to kiss her!

"Once we get back to Portland, you can offer me whatever you want," he said, testing her reaction.

With a noncommittal hum, Emma took another bite of her cookie. Her gaze stayed on his.

"Everything tastes so good in the open air," she commented with her mouth partly full. "If the session ran any longer than two weeks, I'd gain a hundred pounds."

"You'd still look good." Morgan tried to be gallant. Perhaps she, too, felt awkward about exploring their attraction right now. Or worse, pressured, which was exactly why he needed to back off.

"My adoptive mother is chunky," she said. "She's tried every diet known to man, so I suppose I should be grateful we aren't really related."

He pulled a few random blades of grass. "Talking to them might start the healing process for you," he ventured.

She stared at the mountain range with apparent fascination. "Or it might just make things worse."

"I could recommend a counselor who's got a lot of experience with this kind of situation," he offered.

She studied a patch of clover, picking through the leaves with her fingers. "You already know what would help."

"Why is it so important to you?" he asked. "Have you figured that out yet?"

"I have a right to know," she said stubbornly.

Morgan didn't want to argue, not on such a beautiful afternoon, so he changed the subject.

"How long have you been divorced?" he asked bluntly. And whose idea was it? he wanted to add, but didn't.

She went back to studying the patch of clover. "A few months."

"I'm sorry. I've never been married, but I know that kind of breakup can be rough."

"Especially when you don't see it coming," she replied.

The bitterness in her voice made him sad for her. "Want to tell me about it?"

She lifted her head so her gaze met his. "Are we playing shrink?" she asked.

He couldn't blame her for being wary, but he really wanted to know what had happened. "I'm trying to play friend."

Her gaze flickered. "Sorry. I guess I got a little too used to protecting myself from so-called friends."

He waited silently, giving her time to decide whether to trust him. "Don and I decided it was time to start our family," she said in a low voice. "Unfortunately, as I mentioned before, I had two miscarriages."

Morgan resisted the urge to offer comfort. Instead he waited for her to continue.

"We were both disappointed after the first miscarriage, but we decided to try again. When that didn't work, we went to the doctor, who performed a laparoscopy. Before we had a chance to discuss the treatment options, Don decided to book."

Her eyes were dry when she looked at Morgan, but her face was pale. The freckles scattered across her nose stood out. "Looking back, I realized that perhaps I should have seen it coming. I thought we were solid, you know?"

Morgan resisted the urge to curve his arm around her shoulders. Instead he settled for a reassuring and yet platonic pat on her hand. Her skin was soft and cool to the touch.

"Don't blame yourself," he said, even though she probably wasn't expecting a reply. "The signs aren't always obvious."

"No kidding." She took a drink of water from the bottle beside her. "Looking back, I think splitting up was for the best," she said firmly. "A child makes a good marriage better, but it can't hold a weak one together forever."

"That's very insightful," he murmured. "Does it mean you've put that relationship behind you?"

"Absolutely," she said brightly. "Now tell me all about you."

He gave her the thumbnail bio, which he considered to be pretty boring. After he mentioned earning his doctorate in social work, she interrupted with a question.

"Why are you still single? I haven't heard you mention a significant other."

Morgan couldn't hold back a smile. "My mother asks the same thing all the time."

"And what do you tell her?" Emma persisted.

He shrugged. "Depends on how clever I'm feeling at the time."

"What's the clever answer?"

"That she's spoiled me for any other woman."

"Not all that clever," Emma smirked. "What's the truth?"

He figured it was a fair question, given what he knew about her. "I came close a couple of times," he admitted, holding her gaze with his. "You know the old saying, that everyone's looking for someone?"

She bobbed her head.

"Well, I'm looking for *the* one." The sentiment sounded so corny when he put it into words, but that was how he felt.

Emma nodded again. "I hope you find her."

"We'd better start back," he said reluctantly.

The sun had dipped lower in the sky and the shadows were beginning to lengthen as they gathered everything up and Morgan helped her to her feet.

"I hate leaving such a beautiful spot." Emma slipped on her pack. "It's been fun."

She began retracing their path across the meadow. As they neared the shelter at the edge of the trees, she looked over her shoulder as though she was committing the scene to memory.

Exchanging a smiling glance with her, Morgan turned around and walked backward. He knew when he came back the next time the view would have changed.

"Ow! Oh, damn!" Emma's startled cry pierced his reverie like an archer's arrow. She fell to the ground so abruptly that Morgan nearly tripped over her.

"What is it? What is it?" Dropping his pack, he leaned down to her as she lay sprawled in the grass.

Her face was contorted with pain, her leg bent nearly double.

"Oh, my ankle. Damn, damn, damn!" she exclaimed, clutching at her boot as she rolled back and forth on the ground. "I stepped wrong on a rock. I must have twisted it."

"Hold still. Let me take a look." Morgan crouched down and put his hand on her knee in an attempt to calm her. "Come on, sweetie, let me check it out."

She took several deep breaths and stopped her thrashing. "I'm sorry," she gasped, lying back. "How stupid of me."

"It's okay, don't worry about that." He unlaced her short boot, relieved that he didn't see any immediate swelling. While she sat up, he dug a cold pack from his bag and handed it to her. "Hold this on your ankle."

She winced, but she did as he instructed.

"How does it feel?" he asked after a minute.

"The cold pack is helping." She shifted restlessly. "I think I overreacted."

"Give it a minute and then we'll check again for swelling," he said, sitting down beside her. "An ankle sprain can be pretty serious."

"It will be fine," she insisted, handing him back the cold pack and wiggling her foot. "It hardly hurts at all." She lifted her head and looked around. "We should probably get going."

"Are you sure?" he asked. "I can wrap it in an elastic bandage for extra support. If you want, I can find you a walking stick."

"I'm such a baby," she said in a disgruntled tone as she began lacing up her boot.

"Not too tight," he reminded her.

"Help me up, okay?" she asked when she was done.

He pulled her to her feet. If things had been different, he would have wrapped his arms around her and held her close. Instead he put one arm around her waist while she found her balance on one foot.

"Careful," he cautioned, looking down at her bowed head. "Take your time."

Gingerly she put weight on her injured ankle as she gripped his forearm to steady herself. Immediately her leg gave out beneath her.

"Oh, damn. It hurts," she said plaintively as he tightened his grip to keep her from falling.

"Let me help you down and then we'll figure out

what to do next." Morgan held on to her elbows and lowered her to the grass. "Are you in a lot of pain?" he asked. "I don't want to remove your boot just yet. If your ankle were to swell, you couldn't get it back on."

"It's not so bad." She put on a brave face. "Why couldn't this have happened when we were back at camp?"

He ignored the rhetorical question as he dug into his pack and took out his cell phone. "I'll call down there so they don't worry."

Emma's stomach clenched. How could she not have figured that he might bring his cell with him? "Will it work from here?" she blurted.

"It's not something you should count on because you can't always get a signal." After a moment he shook his head. "We're probably too close to the mountains."

As he looked around through narrowed eyes, she slowly let out the breath she'd been holding. "What if you can't get through?" she asked.

"I'll try again over by the lake. Maybe we'll get lucky." After he stood up, he gave her a reassuring smile. "We'll be fine, Emma. I just don't want them to panic."

Alarmed, she watched him walk away. She hadn't taken into account that a search party from camp would surely set out when the two of them failed to return. What if a rescue helicopter was dispatched? Was the meadow big enough for it to land safely, especially after darkness fell?

There were so many things she didn't know. What

if someone got hurt trying to rescue her, or the chopper crashed somewhere in the wilderness on its way to save them?

The thought sent a chill through her that pooled in her abdomen and then turned into a ball of ice as she watched him walk away. She'd assumed their absence wouldn't be noticed until morning, just like in the city, and she had figured they would spend the night here together. By morning, her ankle would be fine.

She leaned back and braced herself on her arms, relieved that he appeared to be talking to someone. Her plan was falling apart, but she had no experience at manipulating people on such a grand scale. If she had, she might have managed to stop her ex-husband from deserting her just when she needed him the most.

After a couple more minutes Morgan put the phone into his pocket and came back to where she waited anxiously.

"I got hold of Derrick and told him about your ankle," he said, looking relieved. "If we aren't back before dawn, he and Jeff will start out after us."

"Dawn?" she echoed.

"There wouldn't be enough time for them to come all the way up here and help you back to camp before dark," he explained as he dropped to the ground beside her. "If you can't walk, we're better off staying in the shelter until daylight than spending the night in the woods."

The image of being lost in a dark forest sent a shiver of panic through Emma. What if he decided to set out without her?

"You won't leave me alone, will you?" she asked, clutching his arm. "I'd be terrified."

Solemnly he patted her hand. "I wouldn't desert you. We're in this together."

Beneath her palm, his forearm was warm to the touch and the light dusting of hair made her want to stroke his skin. She struggled to keep her elation from showing as she looked into his face. Spending the night together in the shelter was a much better idea than trying to hike back to camp.

"I guess we don't have any choice," she agreed softly, slipping her hand into his. "I'm glad you're with me."

Something sparked in his eyes as his fingers squeezed hers, but then he pulled away and got to his feet. "How does your ankle feel now?"

Disappointed by his withdrawal, she shifted the cold pack and extended her bare leg. Cautiously she moved her foot. "It's not sore right now."

Already the sun was heading toward the line of trees to the west. Once it set, the temperature would no doubt drop quickly.

"We need to check out the shelter," he said. "It's not that far. Once you're settled, you can take a couple of anti-inflammatory pills and elevate your foot. That may help to keep it from swelling."

"Okay." She was content to let him take charge. The way he stood over her with his hands parked on his hips and a confident expression on his face while he made the decisions might not be politically correct, but it was certainly sexy.

"I'll come back for the packs," he said as he helped her up.

It was far too late for Emma to turn back now. Carefully she balanced on one foot while she steadied herself with a hand on his shoulder. The feel of his muscles under her palm was such a distraction that she nearly forgot to keep her weight off her injured ankle.

"I must look like a stork," she muttered as she wobbled on one leg.

"Okay, put your arms around my neck." There was a sudden edge to his tone as he ducked his head.

She realized that he planned to carry her. If she had been standing on her own, the thought of being held in his arms might have made her legs go weak. "Maybe I could hobble that far."

"The ground's too uneven," he replied. "Also, we need to get the basics done on our way. Don't be embarrassed. After putting on this camp session for the last five years, there isn't much I haven't had to deal with."

As Emma realized his intention, her cheeks flamed and she gaped up at him in sheer horror. "I can manage on my own," she stammered.

"Oh, really?" He cocked one dark brow. "How?"

It was one more thing she hadn't thought out. "Well, maybe not," she muttered.

"If it will help, think of me as a male nurse," he urged, straight-faced.

She really had no other choice, so she slipped her arms around his neck. When he scooped her up, the world seemed to spin, making her feel suddenly dizzy. She forgot to breathe. Her head was tucked under his chin, her cheek pressed so close against the warm skin of his throat that she could feel him swallow.

"Okay?" he asked as he settled her into his arms.

She loosened her hold around his neck so she wouldn't choke him. "I'm fine," she croaked.

His scent was a mixture of outdoors, sunshine and the faintest hint of cologne. Her fingers seemed to have minds of their own, wanting to delve into the black hair at his nape as he headed for the trees.

A few minutes later, with her once again settled into his arms, they emerged from the descending gloom.

"Now that we've gotten that out of the way, let's check out the accommodations," he suggested, as if they were indeed staying at the Hilton, as he had called the shelter when they first passed it.

Already the temperature was dropping. Emma hadn't thought out the details of spending the night with nothing heavier than their thin jackets, and this deep into the summer the forest was far too dry to risk a campfire.

Morgan shouldered open the door to the small rectangular structure. Fading light came through the single window. Emma was pleasantly surprised to see that the glass was intact.

Morgan crossed the wood floor and set her down on a built-in bench. Next to her was a pile of folded blankets. In one corner sat a small stove.

"There's wood outside next to the building, but we'll leave it for someone to use in the colder weather," he said. "I'll shake out the bedding when I get back so we don't have to lie directly on the floor."

Emma glanced at the worn blankets, wishing she had her sleeping bag instead.

He pulled out his flashlight and shone it into the corners while she listened hard for any sounds of escaping critters. She didn't hear anything.

"For a mountain retreat, it looks reasonably clean," he said, switching off the light. "Someone must have stayed here recently. Even the floor's been swept."

"I'm sure we'll be fine," Emma agreed as she looked around. She'd prefer candles, music and goose down, but this would just have to do.

"I'll get the packs. We might as well finish off the apples and some of the water we've got left." Morgan handed her the cold pack. "Elevate your ankle and put this on it."

While he was gone, Emma studied her surroundings.

Maybe the shelter wasn't so bad, she thought. The walls and the door looked solid enough to keep a marauding bear from breaking in, and there was room on the floor for both of them to stretch out. She was encouraged that he thought they'd be warm enough without a fire.

When he appeared a few moments later with the packs, she assumed he'd taken a detour into the woods. He offered her an apple and one of the water bottles, but she didn't want to risk drinking any more liquid before dawn and she was too nervous to be hungry.

"No, thanks," she said, setting aside the cold pack so the skin of her ankle wouldn't freeze.

"You'll feel better with something in your stomach." Again he held out the apple and water.

"Okay." She set aside the fruit, but she took a small sip of water and swished it around in her mouth before swallowing.

He carried the blankets and quilts outside to shake each of them vigorously. "These will make a decent sleeping pallet," he said when he returned. He folded them back up and tossed them down. "I guess this turned out to be a bigger bite of the great outdoors than you planned on taking."

Emma was determined not to complain. He wouldn't appreciate a whiner.

"It's an experience I'll remember," she said, injecting her voice with enthusiasm and smiling. "And the company is outstanding."

"Thanks." He removed her rolled-up jacket from her pack, shook it out and extended it to her. "Cold?"

She wadded the windbreaker back up and jammed it beside her. "Not yet, thanks."

He sat down on the floor with his back resting against the wall facing her and took a healthy bite of the other apple. His lips were shiny with the juice, his jaw dark with beard stubble.

Fascinated, she watched him eat and tried to read him. Awareness spun out between them, like the web of a busy spider.

He tipped his head to the side, studying her, too. His eyes looked thoughtful and sexy as hell.

"Any tingling or numbness in your ankle or your foot?" he asked between big, juicy bites of apple. "I've got pills in my kit, if you want something for the pain."

Tingling? Not in her foot, she thought, swallowing a bubble of wild laughter.

"I'll hold off on the meds," she replied. "No tingling or numbness, except from the cold pack, and not much ache either, as long as I'm not dancing."

She shook back her hair, wishing she had a brush and some makeup. But wouldn't that have looked suspicious? "Maybe I did just twist it, but I feel like such a klutz."

He shrugged his wide shoulders, such a pleasant surprise out of his well-tailored suit jacket. "It could have been worse." He wiped away the last of the apple juice with the back of his hand and set aside the core. "We've got the shelter, it's not snowing and my cell worked," he continued.

"Are you always such an optimist?" she couldn't resist asking. Until recently, she had looked on the bright side of life as though it was her due. Now she knew to reach out and grab what she wanted or be rolled over like a lump of asphalt.

"I try to be positive." He settled back with one leg bent and his arm resting on his knee. "No one would blame you for feeling a little hammered after what you've been through. Are you coping okay?"

"Right now I'm happy not to be here alone."

His grin faded and a muscle jumped in his cheek. "Me, too," he finally admitted.

Smooth move, Davis, Morgan thought as he fought the urge to slurp her up. What was he trying to do, make her nervous about spending the night in his company?

"Are you tired?" He could justify a comforting hug, but could he leave it at that if she welcomed his touch? Maybe not, so he stayed where he was.

"I'm wide-awake." She shifted on the wooden seat. "Maybe I should stretch my leg out flat to keep the swelling down. What do you think?"

Morgan glanced around the tiny room. They'd be awfully close to each other with her on the floor, but if it would help her ankle… "That's a good idea. You should sit down here."

She held out her arms. "Would you mind?"

Reluctantly he got to his feet. "No problem."

To give himself a moment, he fashioned a pallet on the floor with the folded blankets. When he could stall no longer, he reached down to her.

He was so close that he could have connected the freckles splashed across her nose or counted the individual lashes that framed her eyes. Her pupils were dark and dilated, the irises mere rings of silver.

If he had glimpsed a hint of caution on her upturned face, if he saw or heard or felt reluctance, his shaky control would have held.

"Morgan?"

He had no defense against the welcome in her voice when she whispered his name, or the stroke of her fingers along his jaw. Or the sigh of her breath touching his mouth.

The gentle puff of air might as well have been a match tossed into a brush pile. His good intentions, like dry leaves, went up in a hot lick of flames.

With a groan of surrender, he covered her mouth with his.

Seven

The instant that Morgan wrapped his arms around Emma and crushed his mouth to hers, she realized that she had underestimated the strength of the attraction between them—and gravely overestimated her ability to resist it.

The first kiss they shared was just the way she would have imagined the first hit of some drug to feel—a soaring, forbidden tangle of physical and emotional reactions, all of which she had been so confident she could handle. Even as she scrambled to keep from going under, she reached for more.

They grabbed at each other, hands busy, mouths open and eager. She rose up to meet him, plastering her soft, yielding curves to the hard planes of male muscle. Chest to thigh, their bodies bumped, rubbed and meshed.

Instinctively she curled her injured leg around his calf in order to keep herself from putting weight on it and rising up to her toes. She locked her arms around his neck and hung on tight.

He froze, still as stone. His arousal nudged her, but he waited for some signal from her.

Boldly she traced the shape of his mouth with her tongue and then slipped it inside to taste and tease. His response was immediate and gratifying. A growl worked its way up his throat, his arms became steel bands and he shattered her buttoned-up image of him with another voracious kiss.

Blood roared in her ears like the crash of water pounding a rocky coast. Her hand caressed the rough promise of beard along his jaw. Her fingers circled his ears and plunged into the heavy silk of his hair.

He kissed her again and again. They broke contact for necessary gulps of air and mutual groans of pleasure. Her senses swam, her mind blurred. The bongo beat of her pulse echoed the hard thump of his heart against her breast.

Unlocking his lips from hers, he slid his hands down her sides to her waist, leaving a fiery trail. She resented the barrier of her clothing between his palms and her skin. His grip tightened as though he meant to set her away from him.

"Damn," he growled, resting his forehead against

hers, chest heaving for breath, "I forgot about your ankle. Have I hurt you?"

"No, no, it's okay." Before the truth could spill from her lips, she crushed them to his open mouth. Desperately she poured herself into the kiss, her entire body straining toward him, melting into him.

When he finally lifted his head, she nearly cried out with disappointment. He bent down to slide one arm beneath her knees, the other across her back as he lifted her into his arms.

His narrowed gaze glittered like blue fire from the screen of impossibly thick lashes. His face was all taut hollows and angles, the skin flushed with passion. Between her own hungry gulps of air, she heard his rapid breathing.

"I didn't plan this," he rasped. "My idea was to call you in a couple of weeks, to maybe see where dinner led us."

Hearing his intention was a shock. He'd hidden his interest well. She strung kisses up his throat to his chin, ending with a quick nuzzle and a nip of his earlobe.

"Dinner would be nice," she conceded against his neck. "This is nicer."

"I'll stop. I can stop." His laugh sounded as though he were being strangled, half gasp with a hiccup at the end. "It will probably kill me, but if I'm rushing you…"

"Let's not kill you," she whispered in his ear. "Don't stop."

She licked his bare throat, fascinated by his scent and

taste. Senses humming, blood rushing, she sucked it all in greedily, unable to get enough of him.

He kissed her again, then broke it off abruptly. His body went rigid, back straight, head thrown back.

He swore softly. "I don't have anything with me," he groaned.

"I do." She had a story, too, in case he thought to ask, but he didn't.

Holding her tightly against his chest, he knelt on the floor. His mouth ran over her face, her chin, and down her throat. When he laid her on the blankets and stretched out beside her, she arched against him. Her arms were still looped around his neck, and her body was on fire.

Seducing him turned out to be remarkably easy. Somewhere between his husky murmur of approval when he lifted the hem of her shirt and the touch of his lips to her skin, her thinking blurred and her plan went up in flames like an arsonist's dream house.

This was no time for awkward questions. Not only had it been too long since she had inspired a man's hunger or fed her own, but Morgan's passion, entwined with hers, was too strong to resist. The attraction she felt for him since that first awful meeting engulfed her.

He stripped off her clothes while she fumbled with his. When she was bare of all but her panties, he arranged her arms above her head and sat back on his heels. With a pirate's smile, he looked her over.

"You're ravishing."

His chest was wide and smooth, the muscles defined and his nipples as dusky as two copper pennies. She could have looked at him for a few hours longer, but he came back down to her like a cat after cream.

They rolled and stroked, heedless of the blankets. Dimly she knew he was careful to shield her from the wood floor.

Learning as they went, they gave and took. He purred like a dark and dangerous panther when she stroked him, drank in her cries as she bucked beneath his hand. She thought she could take no more when he opened her thighs wide and settled there to fill her.

Racing, raging, lungs burning and bodies straining, they took each other. Together they spun out of control, shattering everything she thought she knew about passion.

Moonlight spilled through the window as Morgan turned carefully to look at Emma's face. Her eyes were closed, her lashes a contrast to the pale oval, her full mouth relaxed and still so tempting. His body betrayed him with a surging response he would have assumed before tonight to be impossible.

The two of them had followed up that first sweaty collision with a slower, though no less heated, journey of mutual exploration. After a last shattering waltz that left them both weak with exhaustion, they had finally recovered enough strength to fumble back into their clothes before they'd curled together again.

She still slept while he mused over the fact that he, too, had dozed. He should have been outside in the cool, fresh air, cutting a sapling switch in order to whip himself bloody for his stupidity and lack of control.

What had he been thinking, to fall on her like a ravenous wolf when he should have been protecting her from *other* wolves. Not to mention bears and mountain lions.

Morgan wasn't a man used to looking backward. If Emma was willing, when they got back to town they would sort it out and go on from here. He certainly couldn't deny their compatibility, not after tonight.

One kiss and the monumental Davis control had melted away like paraffin.

At least from his point of view, they had more going on than basic garden-variety lust. She was spunky and genuine, a real survivor struggling with a basket full of issues that might have flattened someone else.

She hadn't even complained about her ankle, for God's sake.

She stirred and he peered down at the luminous dial of his watch. There was plenty of time to explore that more-than-basic-lust issue again, since she had come more prepared than he.

"Are you awake?" he asked softly.

"Mmm-hmm." Her hand slid beneath the shirt he'd put back on when the air chilled. "Here I thought I just dreamed you."

His stomach muscles clenched in response to her

touch, and the blood from his head went south in a rush. If he had bet anything tangible on his ability to better resist the sweet temptation she offered, he would have lost.

Through the window, Emma had watched the dark sky over the mountains gradually lighten. Now she sat facing Morgan with her legs crossed while he finished drinking his share of their water.

"How can you look so good after last night?" he asked as he leaned forward to kiss her nose.

"Are you saying that I appear smug?" she teased. "Or just supremely satiated?"

She'd been right. Despite his normal veneer of sophistication, her comment brought a flush to his face. Between the dusky color of his cheeks and the whiskers sprouting along his jaw, he bore little resemblance to Director Davis. More than just his appearance had changed.

Since they had first set off on this hike, everything between them was different. The realization was enough to wipe away Emma's smile and to pull tight the knot forming in her stomach.

She had to be honest with him, but she had no clue how he'd react beyond his initial anger over being deceived. It was nearly impossible now for her to recall the mindset that had actually believed her idea to be a good one.

"I need to tell you something, but I don't know where to start."

His comment caught her by surprise, distracting her

from the statement she'd carefully prepared. His voice lacked its usual conviction, and his expression was grim, but his gaze was level and steady on hers.

Was he about to give her the kiss-off speech? It would certainly save her the trouble of trying to justify her actions.

"I was irresponsible." He brushed her chin lightly with his thumb, then dropped his hands to his lap. "Thank goodness you were prepared, because I certainly wasn't. I'm not used to being blindsided, but I want you to know that as far as I'm concerned, the only thing wrong with last night was the timing."

He bent his head to kiss the back of her hand.

"What do you mean?" So far it sure didn't sound as though he was going to ditch her. Quite the contrary.

"Believe me, honey. Jumping you in the woods wasn't part of my game plan," he said, color still staining his cheekbones. "How do you feel about going back and starting over, once we get home? We could begin with dinner somewhere, like a normal couple, and see where it goes."

Starting over meant a clean slate, she told herself silently. He was a fair person and he would appreciate her honesty.

"It's kind of strange, considering the way we first met," she said, "because I've never clicked with anyone else as strongly as I have with you on so many levels. I'd like to keep seeing you, too. But first I have a confession that could change your mind."

"You're an ex-con?" he asked, brows arched.

"What? No, oh, no."

"Still married? Carrying a torch?"

She curled her lip. "For that jerk? No way."

He frowned. "Involved with someone else?"

She shook her head. "Absolutely not."

"Health problems?" His voice became edged with concern. "Something I should know about?"

"Just what you already know," she admitted.

His expression relaxed. "Bad credit?" he teased.

"Well, not as good as it used to be, but I haven't had to file for bankruptcy yet." She bet his credit was gold-plated, his FICO score off the charts. "I'll be okay once I find a real job."

Smiling, Morgan tapped his chest with one finger. "I can't think of anything else you could say that would make a difference, so go ahead. Hit me with your best shot."

His confidence gave her strength. "My ankle is fine."

His face cleared and he glanced down at her leg. "That's terrific. When did you walk on it? I didn't think I fell asleep, but I must have." He started to unfold his long legs. "Come on. Let's see if you can walk."

"You don't understand." Emma grabbed his hands and held on tightly. Now that she'd started, she wanted to get everything out before she lost her nerve. "There's nothing wrong with my ankle. I didn't injure it."

His grip went slack. "You didn't hurt it?" His forehead was pleated by a frown of puzzlement as he studied her foot as if it would explain. "Emma, I don't get it. What are you saying?"

She gulped, cheeks burning. "I had this crazy idea of seducing you," she confessed in a rush. "I thought if I could get you up here alone, if we spent more time together, that I could—I don't know—worm the truth about my birth parents from you, I guess." She swallowed. "Somehow. It wasn't a well-thought-out scheme. The details were fuzzy."

How stupid it all sounded when she talked about it!

His frown had smoothed out, so that his face looked a little stiff. Twin spots of red marked those chiseled cheekbones and his eyes had turned as hard as chips of cold blue diamond.

She pitied any employee who had screwed up and had to face him.

"Um, I didn't go through with it." Realizing she was babbling, she fumbled and waved her hand helplessly. "I mean, obviously we slept together, but it wasn't because I'd planned it."

She rolled her eyes, exasperated with herself. "I'd changed my mind, but I didn't know what to do about my ankle." Mired deeper and deeper, she ducked her head. "It was wrong and I'm really, really sorry."

"You planned to seduce me?" As he spoke, he shook off the touch of her hands, like someone shaking mud from his fingers.

"Well, it started out that way." She tried out a rueful smile, but he didn't respond. "You were so sweet, and so patient. I knew I couldn't go through with it," she repeated. "Then you kissed me. It was way better than I'd imagined. Everything flowed from that."

"Back up a minute." He shook his head. "Are you saying that you lied about hurting your ankle and that you planned to keep me up here overnight? To sleep with me?"

The ice in his eyes had thawed, turning to twin blue flames. Hadn't she read that blue was the hottest fire? Or was that white? No matter.

"I changed my mind."

"You lied to me." His tone was flat, emotionless.

"Only at the start," she exclaimed. "Like I said, right after that I decided—"

He held up his hand to silence her. "Not another word."

The muscles of his jaw were bunched as he grabbed his boots and shoved his feet into them. He tied the laces with jerky movements, while she waited for him to say something else.

As soon as he had finished, he lunged to his feet. "My God," he burst out, towering over her, "I can't believe you'd stoop so low."

"I was feeling desperate." She scrambled up so she could look him in the eye. Her legs trembled and she felt a little dizzy. "You wouldn't listen to me."

"Oh, well, that justifies everything." His voice was

edged with sarcasm. "What did you think, that I would shout out their names as I climaxed?"

"Of course not! I told you—"

"—that having sex with me wasn't part of the plan. It just happened." He snapped his fingers. "Oh, I forgot. You changed your mind, right between the fake injury and peeling off your clothes. Technically you didn't seduce me. I get it."

She didn't think it was the time to remind him that they'd both been willing. Any more willing and they would have burned down the shelter.

"It's the truth!" she exclaimed.

He turned away, raking a hand through his hair, then spun back around. "What were you going to claim that I did, in order to blackmail me into telling you?"

"What?" she asked. Then his meaning became clear. "No, I wouldn't do that!" Her voice rose. "Obviously I didn't think it through. I just—"

"You counted on me not using my brain, and obviously I accommodated you," he shouted. "I can't believe I was so damned gullible."

She reached out to touch his arm, but he yanked it away. "I said I was sorry. Look, I know you're upset and that we have to start walking back, but can we talk about this?"

"I don't think so." The distaste stamped on his features cut her to the quick.

As she stood facing him, clenching and unclenching

her hands, her doubts grew stronger. Why had she assumed, based on a few hours in the sack with her, that he would believe her?

"I assume you can pack up while I call the guys back at camp." Picking up his cell, he stepped around the pallet. "I don't want them wasting their efforts on a phony rescue."

He jerked open the door, making it squeak in protest. "You'd better get your butt in gear. If you aren't ready the second I get back, I swear I'll leave you here."

The sun had cleared the jagged edge of the mountain ridge as Morgan stalked through the wet grass. For once the sight of the fiery ball failed to lift his spirits.

How could he have been so wrong? He felt like a fool. Not only had he ignored his own personal code of conduct, he had completely misread Emma's character. It had been a long time since he had been so wrong about a woman. In addition, his inability to keep his pants zipped could put both the summer camp and Children's Connection in serious jeopardy if she decided to make a stink.

And to believe that just a couple of hours ago he'd been thinking that he might finally have met "the one." It just went to show how badly a few months without sex could impair a man's judgment.

When he reached the area of the clearing where he'd managed to call from last night, he switched on his cell and stared hopefully at the screen. Thanks to the vagaries of a technology he didn't completely comprehend, the phone failed to connect to the signal. Given his present state of mind, Morgan wasn't at all surprised.

Swearing under his breath, he moved closer to the lake. At his approach, a pair of geese took flight, their wings beating madly as the water sprayed off them. When the droplets caught the light, they looked like jewels.

Several ducks paddled away as they quacked their complaints. Their escape left a wake that scrambled the lavender and peach reflection of the sun-streaked sky.

He tried the cell phone from several more locations, all without success. Disgusted with both the phone and himself, he cut back across the field. He hardly noticed the weeds slapping wetly against his bare legs.

When he got to the edge of the clearing, Emma appeared from around the other side of the shelter.

"Did you reach anyone?" she asked, handing him his pack.

Silently he shook his head as he donned it. He would have liked to start down the trail without speaking, but she stood rooted to the spot. Her cheeks were pale and she looked as though she might burst into tears.

Normally he hated seeing anyone cry, but right now it was impossible to work up a shred of sympathy. He was the victim here, dammit, not Emma. She had played him like a cheap guitar.

"Are you ready?" He clenched his teeth, ignoring

her stricken expression. Was she acting again, playing on his sympathies? Looking back, he had to admit that her trap had certainly worked. He'd walked into it as cluelessly as a rabbit into a snare.

What Morgan hadn't been able to figure out was why, after all that, she had told him.

"Can't we talk?" she pleaded, her gray eyes filling with tears.

He was out of patience—with both her and himself. "I'd advise you to save your breath. You'll need it to keep up with me."

"You're being unreasonable," she cried as he headed down the path into the trees.

Morgan didn't bother to reply. Despite everything that had happened, the accusation stung. He was an even bigger fool than he'd first thought.

Morgan set a brisk pace, but Emma was able to keep up with him despite the dimness of the early-morning light through the forest. And the growling of her stomach. She stared holes into his back, willing him to turn and talk to her. A couple of times he glanced over his shoulder, presumably to see if she was still following him, but that was all.

She had blown it but good by trying to clear her conscience. Why had she thought a straight-arrow like Morgan would forgive her for lying? Her brain must have been on vacation. She should have allowed their relationship to develop naturally and to grow stronger, so he knew her better first.

Instead she had deceived him. Basically she, too, was an honest person. Not that he'd ever believe that of her now.

They had been walking for about half an hour when he came to a stop. "Need a break?" he asked.

Emma lifted her chin, debating whether to apologize again. His profile could have been chiseled from a block of granite as he stared in the direction of a downed cedar.

"I'm good if you are," she replied.

"Great," he grunted as he resumed walking.

Two spirits uniting, she thought remorsefully. Apparently the intimacy they had shared wasn't strong enough to withstand a kick from her feet of clay. Perhaps she was better off finding out now rather than later.

Silently she carried on her one-sided conversation with herself as they passed the same huge cedar tree she had gawked at on the way up. Had it only been a span of hours ago? Looking back, it seemed like a week.

"Hey, guys!" Morgan called out, waving at their would-be rescuers as they appeared on the trail ahead.

Emma's face went hot when she saw the surprise on their faces and realized theirs would no doubt be only the first of a slew of awkward questions she would have to answer.

"Looks like we won't have to shoot her after all," Jeff

exclaimed with a big smile when he saw her behind Morgan.

"Hey, Emma!" Derrick said, setting down the portable stretcher he'd been packing. "How's the ankle?"

Before she could speak, Morgan turned and sent her a warning glare as cutting as a laser.

"Lucky for us, she just twisted it." His voice had lost its chill, but not for her sake. "I couldn't get through to you on my cell," he added, "so we figured we'd meet you partway."

Derrick's smile transformed his homely face. "That's great. Emma, you want to keep walking or do you need a lift?"

The weight of her guilt doubled. "I...I'm fine," she stammered. "Thank you so much, though, for coming up." She barely glanced at Morgan, but she could feel the waves of disapproval coming off him. He practically glowed with it.

"Yeah, you owe us." Jeff elbowed Derrick aside on the path. "Because of you, we missed Cookie's French toast." His grin took most of the sting from his words.

"Don't listen to that hound," Derrick drawled. "We're family here." He extended his hand to Emma. "I'll carry your pack."

"That's okay. I'm fine." Fighting a fresh wave of emotion, she gave him a hug. "Thanks," she mumbled into his shoulder as he patted her back.

"No problem."

Jeff opened his arms and she hugged him, too. Had she really thought no one would notice if she and Morgan just didn't show up last night? She owed the entire staff an apology, one she could never make without embarrassing him even more than she already had.

"Let's get moving," he said with a touch of impatience. "We've got a full day."

Derrick lifted his brows and Jeff glanced at Emma, as if to gauge her reaction. He gave her a reassuring wink and she dredged up a smile.

"Morgan's right," she said, fighting tears. "I've taken up enough of everyone's time."

During the remainder of the hike, she focused on putting one foot in front of the other while the guys chatted about football, work and the remaining activity schedule. In the full daylight, she stared at Jeff's broad shoulders without a speck of interest and tried not to think about Morgan's blue eyes boring holes in the back of her head.

When they topped the last rise going into camp, Jeff and Derrick both stepped aside as though they wanted her to take the lead.

"They're back!" screamed one of the older kids who had apparently been posted as a lookout.

When Emma saw what awaited them in the clearing, her eyes widened with dismay and her face turned hot with embarrassment.

"Oh, no," she muttered, wishing more than anything that she could run back into the forest and hide.

* * *

Morgan nearly plowed into Emma when she stopped in the middle of the trail. As he put his hand out, his first thought was that she had spotted a skunk up ahead.

"What is it?" He peered over her shoulder.

She didn't reply, but he saw a banner strung between two trees. "Welcome Back Emma" in uneven black letters was surrounded by colorful blotches. Handprints, he realized when he narrowed his eyes, no doubt painted by the kids.

As if an alarm had sounded, the campers and staff came hurrying from all directions. They cheered and clapped as though Emma had just been pulled from a mine shaft.

Derrick and Jeff were grinning like jackals as they, too, began to applaud. Morgan leaned closer so he could speak directly into the ear he'd nibbled like a chocolate truffle only a few hours earlier.

"Hope you've got a speech prepared."

Eight

Hands jammed into the pockets of his shorts, Morgan stood back and watched as Emma accepted the tide of good wishes from the kids and the rest of the staff. Deftly she fielded questions about her ankle, pretending relief over recovering so quickly.

He hoped she felt guilty as hell, but he doubted she was capable of that much sensitivity. She had certainly fooled him.

Pretending for the rest of the week that nothing was wrong between them wouldn't be easy, but he was used to keeping his feelings under wraps. Perhaps Emma would have the good sense to avoid him as much as possible.

He realized with a scowl that doing so after openly

seeking him out up until now was bound to whip up some speculation about the real reason they'd stayed together at Johnson Lake. Emma might not care about her reputation, but Morgan couldn't afford gossip to reach the ears of their more conservative patrons. He had no choice but to continue treating her the same as he had before.

Before what had possibly been the best and worst night of his life.

He had to keep his hands off Emma—whether to kill her for putting him in this position or to kiss her again and find out if she tasted as good as he remembered. With that directive, the rest of the camp session was going to drag like the broken muffler on his high school Chevy.

Emma was taking her turn at kitchen KP, spreading peanut butter on enough bread for thirty PB&J sandwiches. Heidi had offered to fill in this morning so that she could rest, but of course she had refused. If Heidi knew the real story, all she would have felt toward Emma was scorn.

She dug another scoop of peanut butter from the huge jar. All she wanted to do was to hide under her bunk until it was time to go home, or at least until the campfire signaled the end of the day so she could go back to her room and wallow in guilt for letting down everyone, especially Morgan. Instead she had to keep a smile plastered on her face, focus on the children and their needs instead of her own shaky emotions and answer endless questions about her so-called adventure in the great outdoors.

"The worst thing would be getting hungry," Cookie exclaimed as he peeled carrot curls for a huge salad. "Did you have to eat any berries or grubs?"

He was a big man with a toothy grin, tattoos covering both arms and a small gold hoop in one ear. There was whispered speculation among the children that he'd been the cook on a pirate ship. When they dared to ask him, the laugh rolled up from his gut like thunder on the high seas. He never denied it.

"We took a picnic lunch," Emma reminded him, dealing another row of bread slices like playing cards. "We weren't gone long enough to resort to eating grubs."

Franny stuck her head in the doorway. "Emma, Morgan wants to see you in his office."

Cookie made a kissing noise with his thick lips. "He misses you," he cooed, waving the peeler.

"You couldn't be more wrong," she said dryly. She couldn't blame Cookie for leaping to the wrong conclusion after she'd chased Morgan all last week. Why hadn't she realized the others would notice her interest and draw their own conclusions?

Franny slapped the doorjamb with her hand. "He's waiting," she said pointedly.

Emma gestured at the bread with her butter knife. "Tell him I'm a little busy, would you please?"

Was he going to kick her out? Since everyone had

ridden up here together, he could hardly expect her to leave before the session was over in a few more days. Until then, they were stuck ignoring each other.

"He said for me to take over for you," Franny replied.

Emma clamped her mouth shut before she could say something she would regret. The situation wasn't the other woman's fault. Franny was only doing what she'd been told.

"Don't you have kids to look after?" Emma asked on a last desperate attempt to stall.

Cookie was studying her with a frown. "Don't worry," he said, reaching over to pat her arm. "I'm sure you're not in trouble. Even if you were, Morgan is very fair. I've never seen him lose his temper, so he's not going to blast you."

Cookie hadn't seen the icy blast of his temper after her confession, she thought ruefully. Giving up, she untied her apron and handed it to Franny.

"Thanks for letting me know," Emma told her. "I'll be back as soon as I can."

"Oh, don't worry," Franny replied, laughing lightly. "Take a nap before lunch, if you feel like it. You could probably use one."

Because of the bags under her eyes? Was everyone here conspiring to make her feel even more guilty, she wondered as she walked slowly down the hall. If so, they were succeeding big-time.

The door to Morgan's office was open, but still she

hesitated on the threshold. His head was bent as he wrote something on a yellow legal pad, making her wonder if he missed his computer.

A wave of longing swept over her as she watched him. Not only had she messed up her chance to find out about her parents, but she had also hurt a man she had come to respect. Beyond that, she refused to analyze her feelings.

"Is there a reason you're hovering in the hall like a truant called down to the principal's office?" Morgan asked without looking up. "Guilty conscience, perhaps?"

There was that word again. *Guilt, guilt, guilt*. He didn't know the half of it.

She lifted her chin. She had apologized profusely back at the shelter, as well as humiliated herself by crying all over the place. She didn't normally wave her feelings around like a flag at a parade and she hated losing control of her emotions the way she had.

Don had told her once, during a fight, that she didn't "cry pretty."

She stepped over the threshold, forcing herself to let her hands relax at her sides.

"You wanted to talk to me?" she asked, ignoring the sharp jolt of dismay that pierced her chest when he looked up, his face blank.

"Shut the door and sit down," he said as he slid aside the legal pad.

She closed the door but remained standing. "You sound as though you're about to fire me," she blurted.

He narrowed his eyes and folded his hands neatly in front of him. "Oh? What makes you think that?"

Blocking the memory of how clever those hands could be, how devastatingly intimate, Emma forced her attention to stay on his face. It, too, brought back painful memories of all the expressions she'd seen there when his privacy screen was lowered.

Desperately she focused on his question. "Believe me, I've been to those kinds of appointments with the boss. My radar can pick up the vibes."

"I'd forgotten about your recent layoff," he said with a frown. "It's never pleasant from this side of the desk, either."

"So you've had to fire employees before?" she asked curiously. He cared about people, so that must have bothered him.

"Of course. As the director, it's my responsibility." He spread his hands wide. "Did you really think I'd turn you out and expect you to thumb it home, just because of what happened?"

She shrugged, pressing down the bubble of annoyance at the way he dismissed the experience. Just a blip, no big deal. "Why did you want to see me?"

He leaned forward, his gaze intense. "I need to ask you a favor."

Other than a declaration of love, it was probably the last thing Emma would have expected him to say.

"A favor, from me?" she echoed, caught totally off

guard by his request. Was it possible that he was no longer angry at her, that he might actually be willing to listen?

"Sit down, won't you?" His face was set in stone, impossible to read.

He'd be one hell of a poker player, she thought ruefully as she flopped into the chair. She was glad she'd taken the time to clean herself up. After their hike back from the lake, she had showered, shampooed her hair and changed into fresh clothes.

Morgan's jaw was freshly shaved, his hair still damp, and he was wearing a striped shirt. If he had deliberately set out to erase the image of her impetuous lover, he'd done an outstanding job.

"I know that I made some bad choices." She swallowed hard past the lump threatening to block her throat. "You have to believe that I changed my mind before we—" She dropped her gaze to her tightly clenched hands. "What happened between us wasn't part of some grand scheme to manipulate you, I swear."

"We have four more days to get through before the end of the session," he continued, as though she hadn't spoken. "We got along fine before we went to Johnson Lake. If we act like something is wrong now, the rest of the staff is going to start speculating about what really happened up there."

He jerked his head in the general direction of the path to the Alpine meadow. "I like to think that this program that we put on every summer actually does some good.

You may not have realized it, but we depend largely on private donations to keep the program going."

"I know that." Emma wanted to duck her head, but she kept her gaze on his blue eyes instead.

"Some of the people who give us money have a pretty conservative view of right and wrong," he continued, tapping his finger on the scarred surface of the old desk, so different from the one in his office at the agency. "I don't think they'd be the least bit entertained by gossip about the camp director and a staff member disappearing overnight so they could roll around together in the woods. Do you think so?"

Nausea slid around in Emma's stomach like cooling grease. She hadn't thought through all the repercussions and whom they might affect. She hadn't thought at all.

"Do you want me to leave?" She hated the idea of running away from the situation like a coward. "I suppose I could plead a family emergency or something. That shouldn't raise any suspicions."

If she could hitch a ride to Sisters, perhaps there was a bus she could take back to Portland.

Morgan was already shaking his head before she was done forcing out the words.

"That won't work," he said. "Jeff has already made a couple of his joking comments about your fake injury and our real reason for going off alone together. He was just razzing me, of course, but your sudden disappearance would only add fuel to the fire."

Deep down inside, Emma had hoped that her offer to leave would spur Morgan into admitting that he didn't want her to go. Instead he had just made it clear as crystal that his sole reason for keeping her around was to prevent any threats to the camping program.

Emma struggled against the selfish disappointment that tightened around her throat like a steel band, making it difficult for her to reply. She longed to reach out and touch his hand, to see for herself if he was as cold as he appeared or warm, the way she remembered.

How could he think of the intimate connection they had shared as just a nasty little tidbit for gossip? His entire demeanor seemed so unapproachable as he sat across from her that she didn't quite dare open herself up to more rejection.

"So what do you want me to do?" she asked, making her tone as devoid of emotion as his had been.

He put his elbows on the desk as he leaned forward. "I don't think either of us has a choice. Try to act the same way toward me as you did before we took that damned hike. Just dial it back a bit, so no one thinks we're actually flirting. Think you can do that?"

Her face went hot with embarrassment. Her subtle approach had made her a laughingstock.

"Okay. I'll try to control myself."

A muscle jumped in his cheek. "Pretend we're still friends."

She wanted to say something sassy, like "I'm not that

good an actor," just to shove some of the mortification she was experiencing back onto him. Instead she locked her hands together in her lap and tried once again to get through to him.

"I've seen how much the kids love coming here, and how good it is for them to feel special, even if it's only for a few weeks," she insisted. "The last thing I would ever want would be to cause problems for your program."

She wished desperately that her sincerity would pierce his armor of icy indifference. She'd seen it earlier—that he felt a connection deeper than mere lust. She knew it!

His face remained immobile, his gaze flat.

"You may not think much of me," she added, her eyes filling with tears that she refused to let fall, "but I'm good at my job. I can talk to kids and I care about them."

"No one's saying that you aren't," he replied, sounding weary. "It's your morals I find troubling."

She felt as though she'd been slapped.

His chair squeaked as he shifted restlessly. "What's your answer?" he demanded.

"I'll do whatever you want." She conceded defeat. "I can pretend that we're friends."

Two long days later Morgan was making a pretense of checking that the boats down at the dock were properly secured. He desperately needed the few moments to himself where his only company was a family of ducks swimming among the cattails.

The strain of pretending a casual friendship with Emma along with the nights spent tossing and turning because he couldn't stop thinking about the feel of her wrapped in his arms were taking a toll. More than once since their return to semicivilization, he'd barely stopped himself from tearing someone's head off when a joking remark was made.

One of the older boys got a laugh at the campfire when he walked behind Emma with an exaggerated limp. The rush of anger Morgan felt at the boy's clowning was a dismaying surprise.

Normally he handled pressure well. But lately it had been coming in droves. A possible huge threat to the agency's reputation had been eating at him since before he came to the mountains. Children's Connection worked with an orphanage in Russia to place babies with American families. An attempt had been made very recently to abduct one of those babies right from the adoptive parents' hotel room.

Morgan had learned of a possibility that the unsuccessful kidnapping attempt had been the work of an organized ring. If the news were to leak out, the resulting publicity could damage the agency's reputation and jeopardize the financial support by its wealthy patrons.

As if that wasn't weighing heavily enough on his mind, he now had the incident with Emma to deal with. He worked with Heidi, a caseworker, at Children's Connection, while two other counselors, Derrick and Jeff, worked at the hospital next door. Normally Morgan trusted their discretion completely, but he was also well aware of the overactive employee grapevine winding through the complex.

Perhaps Morgan was being entirely too paranoid, he realized as he stepped onto one of the boats. It rocked back and forth, sending ripples out over the calm water.

He had worked damn hard to build up the agency's spotless reputation and he didn't intend for a thoughtless remark or a bit of juicy gossip to alter that. His facial muscles ached from smiling whenever both he and Emma were around anyone else. She, too, appeared to be making the effort.

Was Morgan the only one able to read her face well enough to see the strain at the edges of her smile, the shadows in her eyes? How unfortunate for them both that they hadn't decided to loathe each other *before* the hike.

How he wished, as he inspected the oarlocks, that he could wipe from his memory bank the intimacy they had shared. How long would it take to forget her scent and taste, her touch and the feel of her slick, moist skin sliding against his?

He straightened, listening to the gentle lap of water against the old wood pilings. Thinking about her, despite the way she had used him, still made him as hard as the anchor in the nearest boat. He had dated a fair share of women, come close to marriage once or twice, and wouldn't have called himself naive, but Emma's eagerness to spend time with him, her soft purr in his ear and her eager kisses had fooled him completely. Had blinded him to reason and shattered his common sense like a Chihuly glass sculpture.

What Morgan needed was a return to real life where he wouldn't be constantly reminded of one night spent at the edge of the forest near a mountain lake—with a woman who had made him think, for a few hours, that he had discovered a treasure.

No, what he *needed*, he thought grimly as he climbed back onto the dock, was a vacation from his vacation. He allowed himself one last look at the peaceful scene laid out before him with the beauty and serenity of a postcard. Giving the nearest boat an impatient push with his foot, he resisted the urge to wrap the anchor around his fool neck and jump.

When Emma finally, finally got home, walking through the front door of her apartment, relief swelled over her like a welcoming wave.

"Hi, baby," Emma cooed, dropping her purse and suitcase as Posy stalked disdainfully in her general direction. Emma knew from experience that the cat would eventually forgive her.

Closing the gap between them, Emma crouched down to stroke the soft cream-colored fur. After a few more moments of feigned disdain, Posy relented. She arched her back and began to purr.

"That's a girl," Emma murmured. "Sorry I was gone for so long, but I know Ivy was good to you."

Finally Posy's manner thawed completely. She butted Emma's hand with her head as her rumble of pleasure grew louder.

When Emma straightened back up and walked over to the table to sort through her mail, the cat tagged at her heels, meowing repeatedly.

Ivy had left a note next to the stack of bills. "Call me" was all it said.

Emma wasn't yet ready to admit to Ivy that her dire predictions had been right. Not only had Emma failed big-time in learning anything more about her birth parents, but she'd fallen hard for Morgan, just as her know-it-all friend had predicted.

Emma planned to call and thank her just as soon as she unpacked and started a load of laundry. Or maybe she would wait until after she wrote up a shopping list and went to the store.

Meanwhile, Emma glanced over at the answering machine on the kitchen counter. There were several messages, the first two from the Wrights. Even though she deleted them both without listening first, she felt a spark of reluctant warmth at their persistence. As she had recently learned, trying repeatedly in the face of rejection was damned hard.

Head bowed, Emma drummed her fingers on the worn Formica countertop. She had gotten nowhere in her apologies to Morgan, even though she spent the remainder of her time at camp trying to show her remorse.

She'd followed his request that she pretend in front of the others that there was nothing wrong between them. Every time she saw him, right up until the arrival of the bus and van this morning, she had hoped to see a hint of genuine forgiveness in his cool blue eyes.

Before their departure from Camp Baxter, he had thanked each member of the staff with a handshake or a hug. She'd been afraid that a quick squeeze of his hand was all she would get, but she should have known he would play his part till the end. When his arms closed around her for a brief moment and she pressed her cheek against his heart, it nearly killed her to let him go.

When she did, his gaze was already on Sarah, next in line.

"I'll see you all later," he'd said with an impersonal wave before he stepped on the bus with the kids.

As it pulled out of the parking lot with a throaty engine roar and a belch of diesel smoke, she'd had to fight back tears.

Heidi noticed, misinterpreting her reaction.

"Oh, don't start that, girl, or I'll cry, too," she whispered with a sympathetic wink. "I always miss everyone so much. We try to get together at Christmas. Be sure to give me your number so I can call you."

Heidi's warm gesture had made Emma feel like an

even bigger fraud. She doubted she would see her fellow staffers again, not if Morgan had a say. She had lost some friends after her divorce from Don, either because she was no longer part of a couple or they preferred not dealing with divided loyalties.

All of the women had hugged and cried after the van dropped them off in the employee lot for Portland General, where they'd left their cars. Dutifully, Emma had accepted the cell numbers that were thrust at her with good-luck wishes on her job search. She'd promised to stay in touch. Everyone had things to do, so the goodbyes had been mercifully brief, but she'd still felt drained when she drove away. Hands gripping the wheel, she'd stared at the street through her tears, missing them already.

Now her hand hovered over the telephone receiver. She regretted deleting those first two messages without listening to them first. The last one was a call from a temp agency where she had registered for work. Grabbing a pen, she wrote down the number.

Morgan was in the middle of a staff meeting at Children's Connection, trying hard to remain focused with only partial success. The report that Heidi was giving was routine, the couple she had interviewed eager to adopt after repeated fertility treatments had failed.

"What's your recommendation?" Morgan asked when she finished and no one else voiced a question.

"They're willing to adopt a Russian orphan if one becomes available," she replied, closing the file that was thick with papers, including a background screening, credit reports and personal references. "I see no reason not to proceed with a home visit."

Morgan glanced at the circle of faces. They were all wondering how badly their overseas program might ultimately be affected by the threat of a baby-stealing ring.

"Go ahead with it," he told Heidi. "We can't cease operation based on unfounded rumors."

Last night he'd given in to her hounding. He'd met her and Derrick at a local watering hole for beer and a pizza. The place had been crowded with people they knew from the hospital, including a smorgasbord of attractive and available single women.

He had chatted with a redheaded nurse and a long-legged X-ray tech. Neither they nor the busty blonde who sent him a drink had sparked his interest past mild appreciation of the fairer sex in general.

It had nothing to do with Emma, he insisted to himself, nor the feeling of sinking into her heat with her legs wrapped tightly around him and her soft little moans tickling his ear.

A business meeting was the last place to be mooning about great sex. Quickly he shifted his focus onto the business at hand.

"Anything else?" he asked impatiently, pushing back his chair.

Several pairs of eyebrows rose, their owners probably irked at his tone. Just yesterday, Cora had asked him if something was wrong. She had accused him of being testy.

"I do have other work to do," he added, "as should all of you." He heard the sarcasm in his own voice, but couldn't work up much remorse.

"There is one other item," Heidi replied hesitantly. "With Sasha leaving next week, I wanted to suggest that we consider Emma Wright for her position. She'd be well qualified to screen applicants. I think she'd fit in well here."

"Who?" asked one of the other caseworkers as Morgan bit back a snarl of immediate refusal.

"Emma worked with us at Camp Baxter," Heidi babbled enthusiastically. "She was a school counselor until recently when she got laid off."

Heidi's patently innocent gaze shifted to Morgan. "What do you think, boss? Wouldn't Emma be perfect?"

His normally sharp mind went blank. "Uh, I don't think her experience would be a good fit," he stammered. "She's been working in a different field."

His face grew hot as Heidi continued to stare with a puzzled expression. What was wrong with him, he thought. He *never* blushed.

"But Emma's got a Master's. She could learn the job," Heidi argued.

"I can train her before I leave," Sasha offered, oblivious to Morgan's resistance.

"I have her number," Heidi said. "Shall I find out if she'd be interested in filling out an application?"

Morgan felt like a steer being herded into a tight corner. "You're a caseworker, not a headhunter," he pointed out. "It's not your job to round up job applicants."

Heidi's eyes widened and her face went pale. "Uh, I understand." She returned his gaze with a resentful glare.

He felt bad. She didn't deserve his annoyance.

"Is the meeting adjourned?" she asked. "I, too, have other work."

She must give Derrick one hell of a run for his money, Morgan thought distractedly.

"Yes, of course." He glanced around the table. "Thank you, all."

Reluctantly he looked back at Heidi, who was shoving papers into a folder. A spot of color stained each of her round cheeks. "Would you stay for a minute?"

She hesitated and then nodded silently.

Morgan gazed out the window, hands in his pants pockets absently jiggling his change as he waited for the rest of the counseling staff to file silently out of the meeting room. They would probably attribute his short temper to the ugly threats of baby thefts, but he knew the overseas trouble was only part of the reason.

"Please sit down for a minute," he told Heidi as he shut the door.

She plopped into a chair, her indignation justified.

"Tell me why you brought up Emma's name," he said, trying to appear no more than mildly curious.

"She has the right attitude for the job," Heidi replied with renewed enthusiasm. "We can teach her the rest."

She ran her hands through her spiked blond hair. "I like Emma a lot. She really interacted well with the kids at camp. As a school counselor, she's used to talking to parents, and I think her skills would mesh well with the opening here."

"We have other candidates," he argued. "And I'm not sure Emma would even be interested in something so far out of her field."

Heidi leaned forward. "I know there was some strain between the two of you, but I hope you won't let whatever happened color your attitude. She needs a job."

Morgan wasn't sure what to say. Apparently he hadn't been as adept at hiding his feelings as he'd thought.

"I don't think anyone else noticed," Heidi continued. "At least, I never heard if they did." She took a deep breath and slapped her hands on the tabletop. "Maybe you know something about Emma that I don't, but I trust your judgment and I know you'll be fair."

"Thank you for that." His tone was dry. "I'll consider your suggestion, okay?"

"Can't ask for more than that," Heidi said brightly. "Anything else?"

Morgan tugged on the knot of his tie. "Sorry if I sounded gruff."

She smiled as she pushed back her chair. "No problem."

After he'd held open the door, Morgan went back into the meeting room to collect his papers. On his way back to his own office, he stopped at Cora's desk.

"Anything implode while I was in the meeting?" he asked when she was done speaking into her headset.

"Nothing I couldn't handle," she replied.

He figured, in Cora's mind, that covered everything short of another world war. "Would you get me the file on Emma Wright?"

Although she could be opinionated on occasion, Cora was adept at knowing when to keep her mouth shut. Morgan knew she'd figure out this was one of those times. She brought Emma's file to his office a few moments later. Thanking her absently, he sat drumming his fingers on the folder without opening it.

Morgan liked to think of himself as a decent human being. He followed the lessons his parents had taught him, especially those about keeping personal feelings and business decisions separate.

The afternoon sun shone through the blown-glass vase, making a wild pattern on the wall that he looked at absently while he mulled over Heidi's suggestion.

The moment Sasha first gave her notice, he had thought of Emma as a possible replacement. Then he had selfishly dismissed the idea. On an intellectual level, he realized she might be a good fit. On an emotional level, he wasn't sure he could bear to see her on a daily basis.

Apparently he needed to decide how fair a person he really was.

Everett lay in the darkness that night with the covers pulled up to his chin. He liked to picture the pretty house in Spring Heights, but he could barely remember living there before the man came to look for a puppy and took him instead.

Everett thought about telling his parents that he wasn't dead, but they might still be mad at him for being so stupid and scared. They might be disappointed that he was just an accountant. As long as they didn't know, he could pretend they would be happy.

Sitting up in the dark, he threw his pillow across the room as hard as he could. If he was rich and successful, they would be so proud of him that they would forget all about being mad. Before they found out who he was, he had to figure out how to get a lot of money.

How was he going to do that?

"I got the job at the day-care center this morning," Emma said as soon as she heard Ivy's voice on the phone. "The temp agency sent me."

"You don't sound very excited about it," Ivy replied.

"Would you be? It pays minimum wage and it only lasts until school starts again."

With the receiver in one hand, Emma unpacked the groceries that she'd bought on the way home from the interview.

"You'll find something better." Ivy's tone brimmed with confidence. "Have you gotten any calls yet on that last batch of résumés you mailed out?"

"All the districts are facing budget crunches." Emma set the jug of kitty litter on the floor of the closet. She put into the cupboard two cans of the mixed seafood with gravy that Posy preferred.

"At least the temp job will supplement my unemployment benefits," she told Ivy.

"Don't hang up on me for mentioning this again, but you know I'm good for a loan if you need one," Ivy reminded her.

Emma pulled out the crisper at the bottom of the refrigerator. There was a crack in the plastic, covered with tape. The aging appliance was nothing like the fancy side-by-side in her old kitchen.

She didn't miss Don, but she sure missed her house.

Cradling the cell to her ear, Emma stored the rest of the produce she had bought; carrots and radishes, peaches and a tomato.

"Thanks. You're a doll." Emma hated the idea that she might have to accept her friend's offer if she didn't find a decent job soon.

She had been sending out résumés when she wasn't

on the Internet checking out possible leads to her birth parents. Every avenue she explored turned out to be either a dead end or it cost money that she didn't have.

"Have you heard from anyone you met at the camp session?" Ivy asked innocently.

All Emma had told her was that her plan to get more information from Morgan had failed. She was way too embarrassed to tell her friend the rest.

"The only people I've talked to are you and Maria at Kid World," Emma said as she shut the refrigerator door. "I've got laundry to do for work tomorrow, so I'll talk to you later, okay?"

"Congrats on the job," Ivy replied before they disconnected.

Emma had just fixed a turkey sandwich when the phone rang again. Figuring Ivy must have forgotten something, she didn't bother letting the machine screen the call.

"Emma? Honey, I'm so glad to finally reach you."

Silently she gripped the receiver tightly as a lump rose up in her throat.

"Please don't hang up on me," the voice pleaded. "I just want to know how you've been."

A lump rose up in Emma's throat. "No, Mama," she whispered. "I won't hang up."

Nine

After reading the return address from Children's Connection, Emma ripped open the envelope. Her heart was pounding like a Northwest rain shower on a metal roof. Had Morgan missed her?

Had he reconsidered her request for more information? What if it was merely some printed form thanking her for coming to the agency or, worse yet, a belated bill for his time.

When she yanked out the folded papers, her hand shook so badly that it took a moment for her to focus on the cover letter. Her fingers traced the logo at the top. She took a deep breath, bracing herself for disappointment as she glanced at the signature. Her jaw dropped when she saw that it was indeed Morgan's name at the end, written in bold strokes and followed by his title.

"Holy Mother of God," she whispered fervently as she closed her eyes and pressed the pages to her heart. Was this the answer to her prayers? Why else would he write to her on company letterhead?

She sat down on the couch, and the cat jumped up beside her.

"Good girl," Emma muttered, petting her absently. Posy climbed onto her lap and arched against her hand.

Feeling a little sappy, Emma traced the lines of Morgan's signature with her finger. Doing so brought with it a flood of longing, but she couldn't let herself get sidetracked.

Involuntarily, her hands tightened their grip, wrinkling the elegant gray bond. When she could put it off no longer, she blinked hard and began to read.

"What the hell is this?" she cried, her hopes plunging.

Startled, Posy jumped down, but Emma hardly felt the scratches the cat's claws left on her thighs. Struggling with her disappointment, Emma tossed the stiffly worded cover letter aside and read the second page.

Just as Morgan had indicated, the enclosure was an employment application. He was tossing her a bone in the form of a job offer. She was about to rip the paper into tiny pieces, but instead she wadded it into a ball.

"Here, kitty," she said furiously, tossing it to Posy. "Have yourself a party."

The cat laid back her ears at the tone of Emma's voice. Crouched down, she approached the crumpled-up application with the same caution she might a grenade with a pulled pin. Tail thrashing, Posy changed her mind and stalked off without touching it.

Emma would have liked to call Morgan and tell him what she thought of his little joke, but prudence won out over mingled frustration and longing. After one day she already disliked her job at the day-care center. In addition, her bank balance had dipped dangerously low. Conversely, the bills were piling up.

Harder yet, the researcher she'd just hired was unsuccessful in finding a single lead on Emma's parents.

"It's like they didn't exist," the researcher wrote in her e-mailed report. "I'm at a dead end."

Emma wasn't in a position to reject a legitimate job offer, not even from Morgan. If she didn't get any responses to the latest stack of résumés she'd sent out, she might have to swallow her pride and contact him.

"Emma Wright called first thing this morning," Cora said when Morgan approached her desk.

He had been at the fertility clinic talking to one of the managers there.

"She called?" he echoed. "What did she want?"

He had figured Emma would either submit the application, return it in shreds or not respond at all.

"She had a few questions about the opening," Cora

replied. If she recalled the heated manner in which Emma had left Morgan's office the last time, she didn't let on.

"Did she sound interested?" Morgan couldn't help but ask.

"I guess so. She did ask me to mail her another application." Cora grinned. "She said her cat ate the first one."

He wasn't sure how to interpret the last comment, so he merely nodded.

"Keep me posted," he said gruffly before going to his office.

He hadn't yet sorted out his feelings about the possibility of working with the woman with whom he'd enjoyed the best sex of his life, but at least Heidi would be pleased if Emma ended up getting hired. Meanwhile he had a report to read from the investigator doing the follow-up on the attempted kidnapping in Russia, then a meeting with his head of security and the agency's legal counsel.

Emma set the familiar teacup back down on the plaid place mat. Over the years, she and her mother had probably spent countless hours talking at this kitchen table, but right now Emma had no idea what to say. She wasn't even sure why she had accepted this particular invitation after she had ignored her parents' calls for weeks.

"How do you like the job at the day-care place?" asked her mother. She, too, seemed nervous, and her face bore a few fresh lines.

Was Emma responsible for them?

After a hasty though emotional reunion, her father had left to run a supposedly important errand. In reality he was probably doing what he always did, which was leaving Emma's mother to handle an awkward situation alone.

"Even though I've only been working there for three days, the job is frustrating," Emma replied, stirring sweetener into her tea. "I wish I could quit. The facility is decent enough, but there are too many children to supervise and care for properly. Spending one-on-one time would be impossible."

"I suppose the company is trying to make a profit." Her mother pushed her glasses back up her nose, a gesture she made when she was uncomfortable. "Still, it must be frustrating for you to see what's going on. I'm glad I never had to leave you in day care when you were small."

"If I'm ever lucky enough to have a family of my own, I hope I'll be able to stay home with them, too, at least for the first few years," Emma remarked. They both knew it would take more than luck for her to have children of her own.

Her mother brightened visibly at the mention of a possible family in Emma's future. "Does that mean you've met someone interesting since we last talked?" she asked.

"Someone interesting" was, of course, a mother's code meaning "eligible single man."

Immediately Emma thought of Morgan. Interesting? Definitely. Single? Yes. Eligible? Probably not as far as *she* was concerned, unless one were to include potential employer in the mix.

She and her mother had always been able to confide in each other, or so Emma had assumed until recently. The desire to talk about Morgan, at least the G-rated part, with someone who really knew her seemed to climb its way up her throat until it threatened to choke her.

"Funny you should ask," she said with more than a hint of irony. "I did meet someone. He's attractive and single. Too bad I totally screwed it up."

Her mother reached over to pat Emma's hand. "Tell me about him. What's his name?"

For a moment Emma traced a line in the plaid place mat with her finger. Once she began speaking, the words poured out as she described Morgan's character and appearance.

"He sounds too good to be true," her mother replied. "How did you meet?"

Emma took a sip of her tea. "That's the proverbial fly in the soup. He just happens to be the director at Children's Connection. I met him when I went to find out more about my birth parents."

Stiffening visibly, her mother withdrew her hand and squared her plump shoulders. "I know how determined you were to investigate the issue. So tell me, were you successful?"

"Not at all," Emma admitted as she fiddled with the tag on her tea bag. "Except for the same medical report you gave me, their records are confidential. Morgan wouldn't tell me a thing."

"That must have been frustrating," her mother remarked after a moment. "Have you given any more thought to my suggestion that knowing who—" Her voice broke and she had to clear her throat.

Emma felt a burst of sympathy. It was hard not to push back her chair and run around the table to give her mother a reassuring hug. Before she could decide whether to do anything, her mother recovered her composure.

"That knowing where you came from might not necessarily make accepting your situation any easier?" she continued. "What then?"

Emma didn't believe it wouldn't help. She leaned forward, determined to make her mother understand how she felt. "Mama, I need to know where I came from, what my roots are." She took a deep breath as she searched for the right words. "Maybe knowing the names would help to make it all real."

Her mother pursed her lips. "Honey, that part of your life has been closed for a long time now."

"Not to me," Emma exclaimed, slapping her hands on the table to vent her frustration. "I haven't had all these years to get accustomed to the idea like I would have if you had been honest with me." She gulped back a sob. "Why couldn't you be honest?"

Her mother's cheeks paled and her chin wobbled. "I'm sorry." She dipped her head. "We did what we thought was best."

The sight of a lone tear dribbling down her cheek nearly broke Emma's heart. Her own eyes filled and she had to swallow hard. God, but she *hated* this. As much as she resented it, she hated hurting them, too. Part of her, a huge part, wished she could turn back time to before she knew the truth.

No. She *didn't* want that. Somehow the two of them had to work through this, to understand each other's feelings, no matter how painful.

"Mama, do you get what I'm trying to tell you?"

Her mother dabbed at her cheek with her napkin. "No, dear, I'm sorry that we've caused you such distress, but I'm also sad that you don't seem to understand our side. We never meant to hurt you."

Emma felt as though they were going in circles. Biting her lip, she looked away. What else could she say?

Silently she took a sip of her tea as her mother folded her napkin in half.

"I'm sorry," she said again, but this time her tone was different. "Can we try to get back where we were? I don't know what else to say except that you're the daughter of my heart." When she looked up, her eyes were filled with fresh tears. "I miss you."

For a moment Emma sat frozen in her chair, torn by conflicting feelings. Then she got to her feet and held out her arms. "I miss you, too," she replied, her throat clogged with emotion.

Moving around the table, they met for a healing hug. "Let's not go back," Emma whispered on a wave of determination. "Let's go forward."

Her mother dropped her arms and searched her face. "I'd like that and I know your father would, too." She sat back down, cheeks pink. "Thank you, dear."

Emma nodded before she, too, returned to the table. For the first time since she had confronted her parents with her suspicions, the feeling of resentment that had been eating away at her insides like acid began to ease up. It gave Emma hope.

"Perhaps the real purpose behind all of this, if you believe in fate or cosmic circumstance or whatever, was for you to meet Morgan," her mother suggested with a hopeful expression. "From what you said, he sounds like a fine man, so isn't that a good thing?"

Frustrated, Emma went along with her mother's attempt to look at the bright side, as she was fond of telling Emma to do. "No, meeting him was not necessarily a good thing." Briefly she described the two-week camp session, leaving out the part about her plan to seduce Morgan. "At first I thought we really hit it off," she said instead.

"If he's got eyes and a brain, he's interested," her mother said loyally. "Trust me on that."

Her tone nearly succeeded in making Emma smile. "Thank you for that, but it turns out that he has an ironclad rule against getting personal with people he works with."

Her mother waved her hand dismissively. "Maybe he needs a little more time."

Emma hadn't realized until Don left just how little her parents had cared for him. Her mother had made it clear after the split that she firmly believed the cure for Emma would be to find a nice man and get married again. Her attitude had come as a surprise, since she and Emma's father had certainly experienced their rough times.

"Well, I got a letter from Morgan the other day," Emma admitted.

Her mother's expression brightened.

"It's a job offer," Emma continued before her mother could speak. "Kind of ironic, huh?"

"I don't understand," her mother replied after she had poured more tea. "If the man doesn't date women he works with, why would he try to hire you?"

Emma shrugged, wishing she had never mentioned him. "Your guess is as good as mine."

"So you'd be working at the adoption agency?" her mother continued. "The one that has your sealed records?"

"He hasn't exactly offered it to me yet," Emma replied. "He told me about an opening and he suggested that I fill out an application."

Her mother added a slice of lemon to her cup. It was obvious that she was trying to keep her feelings neutral. "What are you going to do about it?"

* * *

Morgan wondered whether Emma experienced a feeling of déjà vu when Cora showed her into his office. He had hoped that flame of attraction he'd felt when he first saw Emma, fueled by the intimacy they had shared, would have flickered out by now. Instead, to his dismay, it burned hotter than ever.

She hesitated in the doorway, looking as though she might bolt. Today her outfit was more subdued than during her last visit, no doubt in deference to the interview.

Her simple gray skirt ended right above her luscious knees. It was paired with a matching jacket over a plain white blouse with a round neckline. On Emma the demure style looked sexy enough to scatter his thoughts like fall leaves in a storm from the coast.

Cora waited patiently by the door. If she had been surprised that he was conducting the interview himself, she was smart enough not to comment.

"Would either of you like anything?" she offered.

Both Emma and Morgan declined. After Cora left, closing the door behind her, he waved Emma to a chair.

This time he stayed behind his desk, hoping the distance would help to keep him focused. As much as he ached to touch the warmth of her skin, he didn't offer his hand. A man had his limits and he was still reeling from the slap of knowing how much he had missed seeing her since they had left Camp Baxter.

God, but he wanted desperately to know whether she had thought about him at all.

"How have you been?" he asked instead, allowing his gaze to skim her face. He couldn't figure out why the particular arrangement of her features, each pretty in itself, was so overpoweringly appealing to him.

Obviously unaware of his scrutiny, she sat down and crossed her legs. Her long, satiny legs.

"I'm fine, thank you." She gave her skirt a slight tug, folded her hands on top of her charcoal leather purse and lifted her delicate brows expectantly.

Her application and a copy of her résumé were on the desk in front of him, the details already ingrained into his memory bank. Just as Heidi had mentioned, Emma possessed the basic qualifications for the position that Sasha was vacating. What Emma lacked in experience dealing with adoption and fertility issues, she could learn.

Morgan sat back in his chair, trying to see past her polite mask in order to gauge her emotions. Dealing with his own personal feelings during an employment interview was entirely a new experience for him, but one he would have assumed himself to be totally capable of controlling. Yet he couldn't seem to distance himself from the woman seated in front of him.

"How's the job search been going since we talked last?" he asked curiously.

Her slight smile wavered before she pinned it back into place. "It's been a little slow."

"I want you to know that I sent you the application because I believe you'd be a good fit for the position," he stated. "Actually, it was Heidi who originally suggested you, but I have to agree with her recommendation."

Emma's gaze seemed to flicker for a moment. "That's very generous of you under the circumstances," she said softly.

He leaned forward, bracing his elbows on the desktop.

"Emma, the letters of recommendation you included with your résumé praise your character." Ignoring the chance for a cheap shot, he weighed his words carefully. If he wasn't careful, he could very well end up looking down the barrel of a harassment suit.

"You and I are in a situation that could be perceived as awkward because of what happened between us, but this is business," he said firmly. "Children's Connection has an opening and you are eminently qualified. As far as I'm concerned, those are the only facts that are relevant here."

He realized that his hands were shaking slightly, so he gripped the stapler sitting next to the desk pad as though it were a barbell.

"I'm willing to put the past behind us if you are," he added.

"I appreciate what you said." Despite her words, she didn't appear entirely convinced. "Believe it or not, I am an ethical person. If you hire me, your trust won't be misplaced, I promise."

"Thank you." He pushed on, going over the rest of the job duties, employee benefit package and starting salary.

Emma's eyes widened at the figure he mentioned, which was apparently higher than what the school district had paid.

"Aren't you concerned that my background of being adopted might color my attitude when I deal with clients?" she asked in a small voice.

"I'm counting on it," he replied briskly. "Since you don't have previous experience in this field, you'll also be attending some workshops and seminars as they come up. You may also be called on to sit in with the support group for adoptive parents that we sponsor. I'll expect you to attend a few of their meetings."

Emma listened carefully to everything he said about the position for which she was applying. Last night she had looked at the agency's Web site, and she was surprised by the extent of the services they offered.

It wasn't easy to hear his voice and watch his face without the memories surfacing, without fantasizing about him, but she considered it a test to discover whether she could remain professional if she accepted the position.

Being away from him hadn't diminished her feelings. The powerful way they had connected with each other, both physically and emotionally, still made her wonder where their relationship might have led if not for her stupidity. If the only possible future connection between them was a working relationship, she had no one to blame but herself.

"Any questions?" he asked when he had finished describing the medical insurance coverage. "If you do come to work here, you'll get an employee handbook, too."

"Are you truly willing to offer me the job?" she asked hesitantly.

A smile crossed his face, increasing his movie-star attraction.

"I am," he said, sticking out his hand. "Are you brave enough to accept?"

She only hesitated for an instant. In truth, her decision had already been made before this appointment. She placed her hand in his, bracing herself for her gut-level response to the sensation of his skin sliding against hers.

"I am."

"First-day nerves?" Morgan asked.

The navy-blue suit he wore with a striped tie and white shirt made him appear to Emma like a sharply dressed banker. No doubt he possessed a walk-in closet full of hand-tailored suits, but to her he would always be the most attractive in a T-shirt and shorts.

She hoped that her own taupe skirt and striped blouse wasn't too casual for her first day of work. When she was here the last time, she'd observed other female employees dressed in a similar manner.

"I'm more excited than nervous," she admitted. "I appreciate your taking the time from your busy schedule to introduce me around." She wanted to show him that she meant to act toward him in a professional manner.

He'd shown up at the payroll department just as she was completing her tax forms.

"It's not a problem," he replied as they walked down the hall together. "Most of my staff seem to be busy getting ready for Heidi's going-away party, but you'll meet them eventually."

"I'm glad to have the chance to say goodbye," Emma replied. "Wasn't her leaving awfully sudden? I hope nothing's wrong."

Morgan paused as they reached the main lobby.

"Derrick was offered the opportunity to go to Africa with a team of doctors. He's a last-minute replacement for someone who got sick. There's a spot for Heidi, too, but the deal hinged on them being ready to leave next week."

An older woman with reddish-gold hair in a chin-length bob came through the double front doors, her face lighting up when she saw Morgan. Emma felt a spurt of curiosity, but she had already warned herself to be on guard against inappropriate possessiveness where her boss was concerned.

"Good morning, Leslie," Morgan said, touching his hand briefly to Emma's back in order to urge her forward. "Here's a brand-new staff member I'd like you to meet."

The other woman gave him a quick hug, kissing the air near his cheek. She was exquisitely groomed, oozing money and breeding from every pampered pore. Yet her smile, when she turned to look at Emma, was very warm.

"Emma Wright, our newest counselor, meet Leslie Logan, our most hardworking supporter and my personal favorite of all our volunteers." So this was a member of the family involved in a long term feud with the Crosbys—Ivy's family.

The two women shook hands. Leslie even smelled expensive, although her perfume was discreet.

"Welcome to the family," she said. She was older than Emma had first thought, but it was obvious from her complexion that she had taken good care of herself. "Morgan is a tyrant to work for, of course," she added with a wink, "but he does a wonderful job running Children's Connection."

"Always happy to crack the whip," he replied with a jaunty bow.

It was plain to see that the two of them knew each other well, which raised Emma's curiosity even more, since the ring Leslie wore sparkled like a Victorian chandelier.

"I won't keep you now." She included Emma in her comment. "I'm meeting a representative from one of the local cell phone companies." Her brown eyes danced as she rubbed her thumb against her fingertips. "They're considering a corporate donation."

"If anyone can reel them in, it's you," Morgan replied. "Are you coming by Heidi's party later? We're having cake."

Emma would have bet she didn't maintain her trim figure with sweets.

"Wouldn't miss it." She switched her attention back to Emma. "I'll talk to you then and you can give me your first impressions of our complex."

"She seems very nice," Emma murmured after Leslie walked away, her heels clicking on the blue and white tiled floor. She certainly displayed the polish and self-assurance of someone used to hobnobbing with the rich and famous. "Does she raise a lot of money for the clinic?"

"It's largely because of her hard work and her generosity that we were able to expand our fertility clinic into one of the best in the country," Morgan explained. "In addition to the financial support of the Logans, there isn't anyone Leslie doesn't know. She's a tiger when it comes to separating the rich and famous from their money."

"So she enjoys volunteering her time over tennis and golf?" Emma asked. "Aren't we lucky to be one of her causes?"

"Her interest is also very personal." Morgan led Emma away from the lobby. "Some people think she's led a very privileged life, but they don't remember what happened to her and Terrence years ago."

"Oh?" Despite what Ivy had mentioned, Emma knew it was never a good idea to make assumptions, because outward appearances could be deceiving. She'd learned that lesson firsthand when she and Don had split up and her friends had been so shocked.

Morgan hesitated at the base of the stairway. "Leslie appears to have it all—money, position, a good husband and a wonderful family. Of course that's all true."

Emma waited silently for him to continue.

"The Logans' first child, Robbie, was kidnapped right out of a neighbor's front yard when he was six years old."

Emma's eyes widened. "That's awful. Was he ever found?"

"The other boy's mother was inside the house and the kid was too traumatized to give the police any help. No ransom note was ever received. I think it was about a year later that the police found some remains matching Robbie's description, but they never caught whoever was responsible."

"My God!" Emma exclaimed, pressing one hand to her heart. "How horrible. I can't imagine surviving something like that in one piece."

"From what I understand, it took years for her to get over it," Morgan replied. "For a long time she and Terrence were unsuccessful in having more children, which made it even more difficult to move on."

"He stood by her?" Emma asked. It was crazy to feel a whisper of envy after what they must have suffered.

Morgan nodded. "They came here and adopted a child. As luck would have it, Leslie became pregnant. They ended up with quite a big family, so their story had a happy ending. In a tragic way, it was their losing Robbie that hooked us up with our biggest benefactor."

"It sounds as though she's made her loss into something meaningful," Emma murmured. In her mind, the only thing worse than losing a child was going through it alone.

Morgan nodded. "She's a very strong woman and she always insists that she gets as much out of her work here as she gives."

Everett Baker lurked in an alcove by the stairs. He had heard every word of the director's conversation about Leslie Logan.

Everett leaned against the wall, clenching and unclenching his fists. Robbie had been a stupid little boy for trusting a stranger in the first place and for not figuring out some way to get away. It was his fault that Leslie's heart had been broken.

Everett was glad the police had found that body so she was able to forget about Robbie and all the trouble he caused. Knowing he was dead had helped her to move on and be happy with her new family.

Whenever Everett saw her, she was usually smiling. Nothing should ever be allowed to spoil that.

"Your office is right down here," Morgan said. As they approached the open door, he poked his head inside. "Sasha must be on a break, but I'm sure she won't mind if we go on in."

He'd told Emma that her predecessor would be here for several days to train her before leaving.

The office was small and it didn't have a window, but that didn't matter. There was all the usual equipment including a large desk with a computer and a phone on its black surface, two chairs, a file cabinet with an ivy plant on top and a side table with a combo FAX and copy machine. The walls were light blue, which harmonized with the tweed Berber carpet underfoot.

"Sorry," Morgan said suddenly as he took his ringing cell phone from his pocket and glanced at the screen. "Excuse me. I need to take this."

"No problem."

As he turned away with the phone to his ear, Emma looked at the blank walls and wondered if it was okay to hang pictures. She picked up a framed photo from the desk, wondering if the child was Sasha's. Morgan had said she was due to have another and planned to stay home with them. The little girl in the picture was missing a front tooth. She was holding a sunflower blossom as big as a dinner plate.

Emma ignored the pang of envy. She would be dealing with many children and parents here, some of their situations happy and others heartbreaking, so she'd better get used to it.

"I've got to meet with someone," Morgan said as he put away his phone. "Walk back with me. Cora can take you around to meet the rest of the staff."

* * *

"I'm not looking forward to this," Emma admitted to Morgan as she clutched her notes and clipboard to her chest.

The two of them were on their way to one of the rooms used for the many meetings and workshops sponsored by the agency.

Emma had really enjoyed her first few days of work, especially since the initial awkwardness with Morgan had begun to fade. He was the consummate professional, treating her exactly the same as he did the rest of the staff. So far she liked everyone.

This morning he had sprung the news on Emma that she would be attending a meeting of the support group he'd mentioned at her interview, Parents Adoption Network. One of the other counselors would moderate.

"We're early." He opened the door to the room and glanced up at the round wall clock. Chairs were stacked against the wall next to several long tables, one of which held water pitchers, cups and a coffeemaker.

"You should have the list of profiles from Cora," he added. "The group pretty much runs itself, so you won't ever have to worry about helping to present a program. All the moderator does is to make sure that everyone gets a turn to talk, that no one dominates the discussion and that no fist fights break out."

He flashed a grin that weakened her knees. "If you

run into trouble you can't handle, either call security or grab the fire extinguisher out here in the hallway."

"Funny," she said dryly. "I'm not worried about that."

He searched her face, and she had to swallow the surge of attraction his gaze always stirred in her. The downside to the tension easing between them was the constant need to remind herself that he was her boss, not her boyfriend.

"Then what's the problem?" he asked with seemingly genuine concern.

"Dealing with adoptive parents is just a little too close to home," she admitted reluctantly. How could he understand the gaping need inside her when he was so darned well adjusted to his own past?

He considered her comment for a moment. "What's the situation between you and your parents? Still not speaking?"

"Actually I saw them not too long ago," she admitted. She and her mother had talked on the phone several times since her visit. By tacit agreement, they were taking it slow.

"Really?" he exclaimed. "Hey, I think that's terrific."

His approval made her feel as though someone had just pinned a medal to her chest. The warmth of his smile sent a rush of color to her cheeks that she prayed he wouldn't notice.

"It's still kind of rocky." She felt compelled to be honest. "We have a lot left to work out."

"But you've taken the first step." His tone brimmed with more confidence than she felt.

The sound of voices came from down the hall. They turned toward the doorway as several people appeared.

"Quit worrying," Morgan said in an undertone. "You'll be great."

After the other counselor introduced Emma to the mix of couples and singles, they all filled out name tags, arranged their chairs in a circle and sat down to talk.

One by one, they brought the group up to speed about what had been happening in their lives. Several of them discussed problems that had come up. As a group, they offered support and shared their feelings.

Emma wondered whether her parents had ever felt the need for a support group like this. Would they have been willing to open up with their feelings as these folks did? Twenty-seven years ago, would a group such as this one have even been available?

Someone coughed, making Emma realize that her attention had wandered.

"Nick's been having these awful nightmares," said a woman with long, light brown hair. "I'm really getting concerned."

Emma glanced down at her notes. Sydney Aston, age twenty-seven, advertising executive, single. Son Nicholas, age five.

"All kids have bad dreams," said a big man with a

florid complexion. His tone was gruff and he kept shifting in his chair as though he was in a hurry to leave. His wife, sitting next to him, seemed to shrink back every time he spoke, as though she was embarrassed.

"What are the dreams about?" Emma asked Sydney.

"Nicky doesn't like to talk about them, but he did say that they're always about somebody stealing him away from me." She tucked her hair behind her ear. "I've tried to reassure him that dreams aren't real. I tell him that I won't let anything happen, but of course he gets frightened. When that happens, I let him sleep with me."

"I agree with Gil, much as I hate to," said another man, eliciting several chuckles from around the circle, which in turn caused Gil to turn bright red. "It's probably just a stage that Nick is going through. Sooner or later he'll calm down."

"I think you're doing all you can to assure him," said another woman with Jenny on her name tag. "The important thing is to let him know he can talk to you about anything."

Again Emma took a peek at her list. Jenny Hall, attorney, age twenty-six and single. She had a son with special needs.

"Thanks, everyone," Sydney said quietly. "I appreciate your comments." She and Emma exchanged glances. "That's all I have," Sydney added.

Several other parents spoke. Most of the group listened with apparent interest. Sometimes suggestions were made. Once, when a father named Chuck described his son's temper tantrum and his own frustration, Jenny, who was seated two chairs away from him, reached over to pat his knee.

"You're doing a good job," she said.

Chuck bowed his head and took a shaky breath, but not before Emma saw the sheen of tears. While he mopped his eyes with a handkerchief, she glanced over at Morgan, seated by the wall. She was startled to see that he was watching her instead of Chuck. When he caught her eye, he winked.

The moderator cleared her throat and glanced around the circle. "As you all know, PAN is organizing a bachelor auction as a fund-raiser. Let's have a report on how it's shaping up so far."

"We've had a lot of response from the singles we contacted," replied a young woman whose tag Emma couldn't read. "Micah Burke from the Trailblazers is interested, as are Jon Hopkins, the computer games guru, and two hockey players." She glanced down at her notes. "Oh, and just the other day I heard back from Eric Logan."

A soft thump distracted Emma. Jenny's daytimer had slid to the floor.

"Excuse me," she murmured as she bent to pick it up, her hair completely hiding her face.

Emma wondered if Eric Logan was related to Leslie. His name sounded vaguely familiar, so Emma filed it away to ask someone about him later.

"If you all don't recognize who that is," the speaker continued excitedly, "Eric Logan is one of Portland's most eligible catches." She fanned her cheeks with an exaggerated hand motion. "He's a major hottie and we're lucky to have him."

"I've seen his picture in the newspaper," Gil's wife chimed in. "He's very attractive."

Gil turned in his chair to give her a disapproving look. Blushing, she shrank away.

"Everything else is running right on schedule," concluded the speaker. "We're going to need someone to get the catalog ready for the printer. Other than that, I'll keep you all posted."

"Don't be afraid to ask for more help if you need it," the moderator said before she glanced up at the clock. "Let's take ten minutes," she suggested to the group. "The coffee's made, Jenny brought cookies and the rest rooms are in the same place they were last week."

Several people laughed as they got to their feet.

Morgan squeezed Emma's elbow gently. "You're doing fine," he said in a low voice. "I think you're a natural. Would you like some coffee?"

"In just a moment, thanks. Excuse me." She was feeling slightly overwhelmed by the emotions that had been expressed so far. These people had opened their homes and their hearts to children in desperate need of both.

They had shown Emma a side of the adoption issue that she hadn't really considered. Before the meeting reconvened, she needed a moment of privacy in order to absorb everything she had learned so far.

Ten

When Emma came out of the stall, the only other woman left in the rest room was Jenny Hall. She was the one who had been so good about reassuring the man who had been worried about his child's tantrum.

"Hi," Emma said with a smile.

To her surprise, Jenny glanced at her in the mirror with suspiciously red eyes as she busied herself washing her hands. Her voice quavered slightly when she returned Emma's greeting.

"Are you okay?" Emma asked.

Maybe Jenny had an issue of her own that she'd not yet had the opportunity to bring up. Emma's notes indicated that her child was handicapped. That would be especially stressful for a single parent.

Jenny's chuckle was unconvincing. "I guess. I'm just being silly," she said with a sigh.

Emma wasn't sure whether to pry, but it sounded to her as though the comforter needed a little comforting herself. With their coffee and cookies, the group could manage without the two of them for a few more minutes.

"Is there anything I can do?" she asked, touching Jenny's shoulder. It vibrated with tension.

The other woman shut off the water and reached for a paper towel. "Have you got a magic wand you could wave to get me out of attending the bachelor auction?" Her tone was rueful.

"Why don't you want to go?" Emma asked. "I've never been to one, but it sounds like it would be a blast." Perhaps she would bid on someone, just to prove to both Morgan and herself that she was so over him!

"I'm sure it will be fun," Jenny said as she turned and leaned against the counter. Her blue eyes looked sad and her mouth turned down at the corners. "Just not for me."

Emma folded her arms. "Want to talk about it?"

"We should get back." Jenny glanced at the door. Obviously she was the kind of person who was more comfortable giving to others than receiving attention for herself.

"In a minute." Emma recalled that Jenny had dropped her notebook when Eric Logan's name was mentioned.

"Should I assume that you won't be bidding on 'Portland's Most Eligible Bachelor'?"

Jenny's face flushed and she looked away, biting her lip. "Was I that obvious?"

"I don't think anyone else noticed," Emma replied. "I don't know anything about this guy. Is there a history between the two of you?"

"Not really," Jenny replied with another self-deprecating chuckle. "Can you keep a secret?"

"Absolutely." Now Emma was really curious.

"I may be too old for crushes," Jenny continued, almost whispering, "but Eric has been my secret love since we were children."

"So you do know him?" Emma probed.

Jenny's gaze shifted to the wall behind Emma's head. "Knew him, but that was a lifetime ago."

By the time Emma came out of the rest room with Jenny Hall, Morgan was seriously considering asking one of the other women to check on them. His gaze met Emma's and she smiled reassuringly.

The silent communication between them alarmed him. He didn't want to feel anything special toward her, but he did.

He was also both proud and relieved over how quickly she had adapted to the job here. Despite her not having access to her own records, he had taken a risk.

Even though they had only spent that one night together, he couldn't get the memory out of his mind. The two of them had shared more than simple passion. It was a daily struggle for him to keep his distance when he wanted so badly to take her into his arms, to explore that connection and see where it might lead.

The other counselor whispered something to Emma, patting her shoulder. Morgan felt like a proud mentor as he watched his protégé call the meeting back to order.

"Who's next?" she asked when everyone had returned to their seats.

A couple of days later, Morgan stood in the lunch line at the Portland General Hospital cafeteria, his mind on the budget meeting he'd just left. Emma, Jenny Hall and one of the other counselors, Laurel, walked by with their trays.

"What looks good today?" Morgan asked after they'd all greeted him.

Laurel leaned toward him. "Not the chicken," she whispered loudly, making the other two women laugh.

"You're only saying that because I grabbed the last plate that was dished up," Emma protested with a grin that lit up her face. She seemed to be fitting in well and making friends.

"You're welcome to join us," Jenny invited Morgan shyly.

"Thanks, but I'll have to take a rain check." The less time he spent around Emma, the less chance of anyone noticing the mooning glances he sent her way. "I've got paperwork to do."

As the food line crept forward, he watched the three of them join two women from Accounting. In his mind's eye, he pictured Emma seated across a candlelit table from him. She wore a low-cut dress as they shared an intimate dinner—

"Who's the new babe?"

Rescuing his tray from near disaster, Morgan frowned up at one of the doctors from the hospital staff. Although Stevens was a gifted surgeon, he had a reputation among the nurses as a skirt-chasing jerk. It was a reputation he wore like a merit badge.

"I beg your pardon?" Morgan longed for an excuse to break off the conversation.

Instead the other man cut deftly into the line behind him.

"The sweetie in green." Stevens gestured in Emma's direction with his bottled water before downing a hefty swallow. "She must be new. Is she single?"

"From what I've heard, that's not a big consideration of yours," Morgan replied dryly.

He had no respect for someone who used his position at the hospital as a way of running his own personal dating service.

Apparently the surgeon was too arrogant to notice that Morgan had turned away from him. "Don't get your shorts in a knot," he drawled. "Just tell me."

Morgan's resistance would probably spike Stevens's interest even more, he reasoned. He couldn't resist looking over his shoulder. "And you'd back off?"

Dr. Stevens leaned closer, his fancy cologne making Morgan want to sneeze. "Hell, no. I'd just know my competition."

Morgan was saved a reply by one of the nurses, who had a reputation of her own. Thrusting out her chest, she gave him a smoldering glance through her bright-green eyes framed in black.

Her expression altered to one of pleading when she turned to Stevens.

"Are we still on for tonight?" she purred with a flutter of her eyelashes.

The line moved forward, so Morgan didn't hear the doctor's reply. With a quick glance at Emma, who was still seated at the nearby table, Morgan slid his tray up to the cashier's station. As soon as he'd paid for his lunch, he went straight to the bussing station and dumped it.

The image of Emma spending time with someone like the playboy surgeon had completely spoiled Morgan's appetite.

In another part of the cafeteria, Everett sat at one of the small tables with Nancy Allen, the nurse who worked in the emergency room. He hated the idea of trying to take advantage of her, but Charlie had been pressuring him for names.

Everett was a little afraid of him. Charlie had a ruthless side that Everett hadn't noticed when they first met at his favorite hangout. Charlie had a plan to make some easy money and he'd been willing to include Everett. Now he had to do his part.

It was easy to steer Nancy around to what he needed to know. She liked talking about the babies.

"I've been blabbing your ear off," she said with a nervous laugh. "It can't be very interesting for you to hear about all the time I spend in the nursery."

Everett couldn't figure out why a woman as friendly and nice as Nancy would look twice at someone like him. He never knew what to say or how to act, but she seemed to like him anyway.

"I'm not bored," he protested. "It's nice that you like babies. You'll be a good mother."

She wouldn't get angry and slap her kids, just because they were cold or hungry. Not like Joleen, who only cared about her next drink.

Nancy's smile widened in response to his comment. Her cheeks turned pink. "I've always dreamed of having a family of my own," she said softly. "Not right away, of course, but someday in the future." She fluffed her hair with her fingers. "What about you?" she asked. "Do you want children?"

"I haven't thought about it." He must have sounded too impatient, because her blush deepened and her smile faded.

Nervously he stirred the bowl of turkey noodle soup in front of him. He was no good at interrogating someone, but Charlie had been insistent.

"Tell me again about that woman you were talking to," he urged, nearly stuttering, "the one who told you her boyfriend took off right after she said she was pregnant. What was her name?"

"Jane Bryson," Nancy replied, her smile returning. "Jane already has two other children, but her new baby girl is just precious. She already has a few wisps of hair, so I just know she's going to be blond, like her mother."

A wave of relief washed over Everett. Charlie would be pleased. He said Caucasian babies were worth the most money because so many people wanted them.

"I'm probably not the best person for you to be talking to," Emma said to the tall, tanned doctor. She recognized him from the cafeteria. He had spoken to her a couple of times there.

Now Dr. Stevens stood in her office doorway in his scrubs, leaning against the jamb with his arms folded across his chest.

"I disagree," he replied with a smile that showed off his dimple, as well as his even white teeth. "You're exactly the person I should be talking to."

His skin and hair had the look of being well maintained, making Emma suspect that he might be older than he first appeared. The long-fingered hand resting on the door frame sported a college ring with a dark stone. His other hand was bare.

"I've only been working here for a couple of weeks, so I don't know a lot about the adoption process yet," she explained. "I'd be happy to give your friend's name to one of the other counselors, if you'd like."

Except for being mildly flattered by his attention, she hadn't given him a thought until he showed up full of questions.

"Maybe I don't want to ask one of the other counselors," he drawled as he turned up the wattage of his charm.

Understanding dawned slowly, along with the realization that the handsome doctor didn't tempt her in the least. What was wrong with her?

"Maybe you and I could discuss the subject further over dinner this evening," he pressed. "What do you say?"

"I'm afraid I can't." She didn't have to think about it. "I've already got plans." No reason to elaborate and tell him they were nothing more than going home to feed her cat.

"Tomorrow night?" he asked. "After that I'm jammed up."

Was that a not-so-subtle hint that he was giving her one last chance? God, she hoped so.

Suddenly Morgan appeared in the doorway behind the other man. "Harassing my staff during work hours, Stevens?" he asked lightly.

Unfolding his arms, the surgeon turned abruptly. "Just getting some info for a friend." His tone was less charming, more businesslike.

Morgan looked past him at Emma, making her wonder if she looked as uncomfortable as she felt. How much had he overheard? Did he think the tête-à-tête was *her* idea?

"Something I can help you with?" he asked Stevens. "Emma's pretty busy."

The doctor gave her a long, slow wink. "I'll talk to you later."

"Okay." She couldn't very well tell him not to bother when her boss was standing by wearing a disapproving scowl.

After he left, Morgan walked into her office. Dismay coursed through her. All the attraction that had been missing when she looked at Dr. Stevens sizzled through her now. It was a struggle to hide it behind a professional smile.

"What can I do for you?" she asked brightly, tucking her tightly clasped hands in her lap.

"Dammit, Emma," he responded through clenched teeth before he broke off abruptly to rake a hand through his hair. "I'll talk to you later." Without giving her a chance to say another word, he spun on his heel and stalked out of her office.

What had just happened here, she asked herself silently. Was she in some kind of trouble?

She took several calming breaths. Of course not. She had done nothing wrong.

Morgan walked past Cora's desk without even glancing at her. What he needed was a hard workout in the exercise room, but there was too damned much work piled on his desk for him to take the time.

What he needed, really needed, he thought grimly as he closed the door to his office behind him, was either a lobotomy or a night with a thousand-dollar hooker. Neither one, he knew in his gut, was going to do a damn thing toward erasing his feelings for Emma.

He threw himself into his leather chair. His choice was a simple one that he'd realized when he saw Stevens sniffing around her like a bull elk in rutting season.

Either Morgan controlled the urge to erect a razor-wire barrier in front of her door and accepted the fact that all the single men who worked here were going to notice her, or he went after her himself.

He'd better damned well make up his mind, which he was going to do before he blew it completely and beat the crap out of someone for looking at her.

He was still in a foul mood the next day after tossing and turning most of the night. At lunch he sat down at an empty table with a sandwich he didn't want. Halfway across the room, Emma was eating with a small group of women.

Feeling like a damned stalker, Morgan kept sneaking glances at her. In a room filled with attractive women, she was the only one who interested him.

Was the small group talking about the men in their lives? His own prurient interest made him cringe. He was a sick, sick man.

Emma had a right to be interested in anyone she wanted, but the idea of her being attracted to someone like Stevens made bile slosh around in Morgan's gut like the cafeteria sludge they called coffee. As he swallowed hard, she and one of the other women, still chatting, bussed their trays and left the cafeteria.

The moment he caught himself sliding down in his chair in order not to be noticed, Morgan's decision was made.

When Emma concluded her preliminary interview with a couple who were interested in adopting a baby from Russia, she circled her desk and shook both their hands.

"Thank you so much for coming," she said, handing them each a business card to go along with the brochure they had reviewed together. "If you have any questions at all, be sure to contact me and I'll find the answers for you."

The couple, both in their thirties, already had one adopted child. When they left her office, the man's arm was curved around his wife's waist.

Emma sat back down and stared blankly at the framed Portland Rose Festival poster she'd hung on the wall. One of the few difficult aspects to this job was constantly dealing with happy couples. Sometimes Emma felt like the only single on Noah's ark.

"Daydreaming on company time?"

Morgan's voice made her entire body jerk with surprise. Blushing, she looked up to see him leaning against the door frame in much the same way as Dr. Stevens had yesterday. Her reaction to the two men was, however, poles apart.

When the surgeon had shown up, her initial mild feeling of flattery was quickly overshadowed by annoyance for being interrupted. Now Morgan was here. Even though he was her boss and the director of the clinic, and even though she was growing more accustomed to seeing him on a daily basis, her body persisted in reacting as though her former lover and the man she couldn't forget was coming back to claim her.

"I was thinking about my last clients," she replied calmly as she folded her hands on her desk. "What can I do for you?"

Morgan surprised her by scowling. "There's something we need to discuss." His tone was clipped. "Would you have time to stop by my office before you leave today?"

Though he had worded it as a request, she didn't get the impression that refusing was an option. Did he intend to fire her?

"Of course." She lifted her chin. Since he wasn't smiling, neither did she. "Five o'clock?"

"Fine, I'll see you then." For a moment he stood in the doorway gazing down at her through narrowed eyes, as though he intended to say something more. Instead, with a nod, he turned and left.

Emma was left to wonder why he wanted to see her. In case her initial suspicion was correct, she set about completing her work. To that end, she switched her computer to the pertinent screen and set up a file for the couple she had just interviewed.

She expected the afternoon to crawl by, but instead it flew. After she had saved her last report and looked at her watch, she was surprised to see that she had barely enough time to freshen her lip gloss before walking to Morgan's office. Gathering up her determination, she logged off her computer and pushed back her chair.

When she approached the reception area a few moments later, she was surprised to see that Cora's chair was empty, her desk cleaned off and her monitor on screen saver. It had been Emma's impression that the other woman never left early.

She peered around the corner to see that the door to Morgan's office stood open. She felt as though she were about to enter the dragon's lair. Tucking her purse beneath her arm, she sucked in a deep breath, eager to get this meeting over, no matter the outcome.

When she reached the doorway, she recognized Morgan standing at the window with his back to her. His tan linen suit jacket hung over the nearby chair and his hands rested on his narrow hips. He seemed to be engrossed in the view.

"Excuse me," she said softly, not wishing to startle him.

When he turned around, his expression was considerably more welcoming than she had expected from their earlier exchange.

"Emma!" he exclaimed as though he'd forgotten all about his summons. "Welcome. Come on in."

"Where's Cora?" she asked warily.

"She had to leave, something about one of the kids." Just as he had the first time Emma had been here, he waited until she sat down and then he took the chair facing her. She had no idea if that was a good sign or not, so she held her purse in a death grip on her lap as she waited to hear what he had to say.

"How have you been doing?" he asked. "Any problems?"

She leaned forward. "I love this job," she said. "Everyone here is wonderful. I enjoy the work. As I learn more, I think I can make a difference."

When he remained silent, she babbled on. "If you've heard any complaints, I hope you'll be up front with me. Give me a chance to fix whatever is wrong."

For a long moment, Morgan just looked at her. "Is that what you think this is about?" he finally asked. "Some kind of progress report?"

Puzzled, she sat back in her chair. "Well, isn't it?"

Instead of answering her, he surged to his feet and shut the door firmly.

Dread curled in Emma's stomach as she waited for him to fill her in. He rested his butt against the edge of his desk, his hands braced on either side of him and his legs stuck out in front of him. For the first time, it registered on her radar that his tie was missing and the sleeves of his striped shirt were rolled halfway up his forearms. His hair looked as though he'd run his fingers through it repeatedly.

"If I wanted to talk to you about work, I wouldn't have asked you to come in when you were done," he said. "The workday ended five minutes ago."

He straightened up and began prowling around the room in an uncharacteristic gesture of nervousness. "Are things improving with your folks?"

She nodded, puzzled by his obvious restlessness. "Sure. They love me. I'm dealing with the realization that they did what they thought was right. I don't agree with what they did, but I'm trying to accept it."

He appeared pleased when he nodded. "And being adopted?" he probed. "Have you accepted that?"

"I've been working with someone. She's got a lot of experience in ferreting out people's birth records."

Now that Emma had a steady job, the search was back on. "She hasn't discovered anything yet, but I'm not giving up."

"Ah, Emma," he sighed. "Whatever you're paying, I'm afraid it's a waste of money."

"Well, it's my money."

The silence stretched between them. She tried to accept the fact that it was no doubt far too late for the two of them to be anything more than colleagues. What she really wanted to do was to throw her arms around him.

"I don't blame you for not telling me what you know," she said instead, fiddling with the catch on her purse. "If nothing else, working here for the past three weeks has helped me to understand that."

Even though she wasn't looking directly at him, she could sense his sudden tension. She raised her head, surprised at the intensity of his gaze.

"Are you sure?" he asked, his voice rough. "You don't still resent me for that?"

"No," she repeated. "Do you still resent me for what I tried to do? I told you the truth. What happened between us..." A sudden swell of emotion blocked her throat, closing off her ability to continue on. "Well, no matter."

"You mean when we made love?" he asked softly as he bent down so that his face was close to hers.

"Yes," she choked, tears filling her eyes. Being so near to him was sweet agony. Before he had become her boss, he had stolen her heart.

"Emma," he rasped, reaching out to lift her chin with one finger.

When she looked up, she knew from the stark hunger in his gaze that he meant to kiss her. He pulled her to her feet and straight into his arms.

With his face mere inches from hers, he hesitated. "Emma, is this what you want?"

Would he resent her later for tempting him to cross the line, right in his own office? Emotions in turmoil, she placed her hands on his chest. Should she welcome his embrace or push him away?

Helpless to resist, she tipped back her head. "You're what I want."

Eleven

When his arms closed around her, the firm muscles of Morgan's chest felt so good beneath Emma's palms that it was almost more than she could do to resist. All she wanted was to melt against him, but she knew with sharp clarification that giving in to this momentary impulse could cost them both later.

She refused to be the reason for him to feel guilty or regretful.

"No," she said, "you've misunderstood. I'm sorry, but this isn't a good idea."

He froze. His arms fell to his sides and he closed his eyes as though he were in pain.

"You're right, of course," he groaned, raking his fin-

gers through his hair. "I don't know what I was thinking. Hell, I *wasn't* thinking at all."

"Don't beat yourself up." She struggled to keep her
voice light, to keep her eyes free from tears. "It was a momentary lapse, an impulse. Please don't think I would ever
tell anyone or cause you any problems because of it."

If she didn't get out of here in the next thirty seconds,
she was going to jump him. Her hormones were raging,
her body screaming. "I would never do that."

"What are you saying?" His eyes were dark with
some emotion she couldn't read. Frustration? Anger at
her for tempting him?

"I know how you feel about fraternizing with the
help," she stormed as her own frustration boiled over to
match his. "Don't beat yourself up for making a pass,
okay? It happens."

A muscle jumped in his cheek. "Is that how you see
it, as some kind of cheap pass?"

Jeez, he looked ready to explode.

"No," she cried. "That's how I figure *you* see it. I
won't have you blaming yourself for breaking that high-
and-mighty code of honor you prize so highly. Just so
you know, the help wasn't unwilling, okay? She wanted
to grab you by the ears and kiss you!"

Mortified by what she'd just admitted, she scooped up
her purse. "I've got to get out of here," she muttered, heading for the door. "Firing me or whatever the hell you had
in mind will have to wait until office hours tomorrow."

* * *

As soon as Emma got home, she took a hot shower, as though that could wash away the memory of what a fool she'd made of herself in Morgan's office. All she had meant to do was to put him at ease, but instead she had succeeded in letting him know how much she ached to be with him.

Poor guy! Because of her, he'd probably never ask an employee a personal question again.

The weather had shifted today, taking one of those detours from summer that the northwest was known for. The sky outside her bedroom window was overcast. Despite the ten-degree temperature drop, her apartment was stuffy from being closed up all day. She pushed the back window open but left the draperies shut for privacy.

If she still had a job tomorrow, she might start hunting for a nicer place. Out by the hospital complex were several newer high-rises. But right now the last thing she wanted to dwell on was real estate.

After she dried herself off from her shower, she opted out of getting dressed again. Instead she slipped into clean undies and a short terry-cloth robe.

Although the scene with Morgan had ruined her appetite, she figured that she'd better eat something. After popping a frozen dinner into the microwave, on loan from her mom, she poured a glass of iced tea.

The bell from the oven sounded at the same time that someone knocked on her door. It was the right time of day for either a salesman or a kid peddling candy to raise money for soccer. Good thing chocolate didn't tempt her unless it was laced with peanut butter.

Curious, Emma looked through the peephole. All she could see was a bouquet of daisies, so she hesitated with her hand on the knob.

Ivy always called before she came by and she was more likely to bring pizza than posies. Maybe it was Emma's dad. He was big on giving her mom flowers all the time.

Or maybe a stranger was trying to trick her. She slipped the security chain on the door, but she knew from watching Oprah when she'd been out of work how easily it could be broken if someone was really determined. Perhaps the Rose City was under siege from some deranged man who got into the apartments of women living alone.

Emma could be the next victim of some serial bouquet bandit, or worse. The only things the women at her lunch table had buzzed about today was the shoe sale at Nordstrom's, the new Spider-Man sequel playing at the Cineplex and the unattached nurse from the fertility clinic who was obviously pregnant.

As Emma hovered by the door with her hand on the knob, debating her choices, the knock sounded again. This time it was louder, making her jump.

Feeling vulnerable in her robe, she sidled closer and peeked out a second time. As though her caller had realized his error in blocking her view with flowers, he moved them so she could identify him.

When she did, her heart climbed into her throat and stayed there, thudding louder than any knock on the door ever could. Swallowing hard, she nearly collapsed against the panel, afraid to draw the obvious conclusion for fear of letting herself in for a major disappointment.

She clutched at the fabric of her robe. If she took the time to grab some clothes, he might give up and leave and she didn't have either his cell number or his address.

Sucking in a deep breath, she freed the chain and stuck out her head. He was already walking away, still dressed in the tan slacks and striped shirt he'd worn to work.

He turned when he heard the door open.

"I'd given up," he said as he faced her, still holding the daisies. "I figured you must have gone out."

She was shaking so hard that her teeth nearly rattled. She had to bite her tongue to keep herself from telling him that he would never have to give up on her again, if only he would give them another chance.

What if that wasn't why he was here?

"On your way somewhere?" she asked, looking pointedly down at the flowers. "Need some water for those?"

He didn't smile as he stepped closer. With one hand braced on the door frame, he leaned down, his gaze riveted on Emma's mouth.

Heat flashed through her. In half a heartbeat, she wanted him as badly as she had back at the office.

"I haven't been able to get you out of my head," he growled, sounded defeated. "Let me in, Emma, please."

Wordlessly she stepped out of the way. He walked past her, shut the door and tossed the bouquet of daisies onto the coffee table. Then in one swift movement he turned and wrapped his arms around her, lifting her completely off the floor.

She held him close and whispered, "I missed you."

"You're so beautiful," he said hoarsely. "I hope you know that this has nothing to do with work or job security. Or— Oh, hell, I can't think what else. If you want me to go—"

Emma pressed a finger to his lips, stopping the flow of words. "I know all that," she replied. "Now shut up and kiss me before I burst into flames."

For the first time since that night in the cabin, Morgan's expression relaxed into an unabashed grin. Tipping his head, he complied with her urgent request.

He kissed Emma ravenously, and she gave as good as she got. With his body pressed to hers as close as paint on a fender, he walked her toward the couch. They bumped against it and he set her down. She freed the buttons on his shirt and started on his belt while he kicked off his loafers and came back to her mouth.

He grabbed handfuls of her robe, pulling it up until his fingers reached her skin. In seconds they had stripped each other bare, grasping and groping as they fell together onto the couch. Emma's last coherent thought before her mind shut down was the daisies. They'd wilt for sure without water. She wrapped her legs around Morgan as he shifted, trying to protect her body with his as they slid to the floor in a tangled heap.

"Would you believe me if I said that's not why I came here?" he asked. They still lay on the floor with his arm beneath her head as Posy watched them from a nearby chair.

"Right now I'd probably believe whatever you told me," Emma replied. Her hand rested on the smooth skin of his bare chest. Beneath her palm she could feel the steady beating of his heart. Good thing her front curtains were shut, or the kid selling candy might have gotten an eyeful.

She sat up and reached for her robe while he pulled on his clothes. Despite her brave words, she was terrified that he'd only come by for some quick sex and now he meant to leave.

"Why did you show up at my door?" she asked once they were seated on the couch.

He took her hands in his. "I made a mistake."

Her heart shot right down to her toes. "Excuse me?" What if he'd only intended to bring her some paperwork and gotten sidetracked?

He must have seen her go pale, because he tightened his grip.

"I should have listened, back at the cabin, but I was feeling duped and stupid. I came over here to suggest that we start over. Drinks and dinner."

Gradually the meaning behind what he was saying sank in. "Drinks and dinner?" she echoed, returning his smile. "How about soda and frozen pizza? It's all I've got to offer until payday."

They had to talk. Morgan refused to get sidelined again.

"Come here for a moment," he said, taking her hand when she stood up. "The pizza can wait. Hell, I'll take you out if you'd like, anywhere you want to go." With his free hand, he patted the worn couch cushion next to him. "Before anything else, please sit down. I have something to say."

For a moment she hovered, wide-eyed. Then, biting her lip, which was already swollen from his kisses, she perched on the other end of the couch, looking as though she might bolt any second.

If he had completely misread the situation and all she really wanted was occasional, mind-blowing, gear-stripping sex, as in "friends with privileges," he would have to change her mind. A man could sure as hell find himself in a worse situation, perhaps, but he wanted more.

"We've probably got more strikes against us than any two people who were thrown together on a reality television show," he began. "We haven't always been fair with each other, or completely honest. We started out on the wrong foot, we took a detour into the woods, and I wouldn't listen or give you my trust when you asked for it. Now we've tossed another complication into the mix because you've come to work for me."

"When you rack it all up like that, it sounds pretty overwhelming," she agreed with a sad little shiver to her voice. "Don't blame yourself. You had every right to hate me, but you offered me a job instead."

"I could never hate you." He reached over and took her hand. "You're brave and funny and smart. You've been through a lot, but you're still standing. You haven't lost your smile."

His grip tightened and he figured it was time to take a chance for the first time in his well-ordered life.

"The truth is, I can't stop thinking about you," he admitted. "I want more than the occasional glimpse in the hall or the cafeteria."

He took it as an encouraging sign when she gulped and her eyes filled with tears. "You want to come over once in a while?" she asked.

His nerves were already raw. The implied insult behind her question smacked him alongside the head, followed immediately by a wave of righteous anger that made him leap to his feet as he wrenched loose of her hand.

"If you can't think more of me than that, at least think more of yourself," he blazed.

She popped up beside him with her chin thrust out. "Don't you dare yell at me, just because I put what you want into words that I didn't bother to dress up with a bow."

His anger cooled as quickly as it had flashed through him.

"It's not some secretive affair that I'm after," he said, struggling to lower his voice. "I want to start over again with you, to put behind us the mistakes we've both made, if you're willing. And, God help me, to stay out of the sack, if we can manage it, while we get to know each other better in other ways."

The astonished expression on her face cheered him up so much that he couldn't resist a grin. "If that doesn't work," he added, "we can go back to your scenario, the one where we sneak around and meet for sweaty sex in seedy motels."

Emma's lips curved into a smile. "I never said a word about seedy motels, but I suppose we could add that part if you want."

"Are you telling me that you're willing to give me another chance and see where this leads?" he asked hopefully.

Emma looped her arms around his neck and leaned into him, stirring an immediate reaction below his buckle. "I am," she said. "Before we start your plan, could we go back over the part about sweaty sex one more time?"

"What do you think?" Emma asked, twirling around before the cat sitting on the foot of her bed.

If Posy was impressed by the new pale blue slip of a dress, she hid it well behind her unblinking stare.

Since that first evening at Emma's apartment, she and Morgan had spent every moment they could getting to know each other. Although they tried not to be obvious, rumors were flying at Children's Connection. Morgan didn't seem to care.

"Too many google-eyed stares," he'd said to her with a grin and a shrug. "Try to keep 'em under control, sweetie."

Now that she and her parents were not only back on speaking terms, but making genuine progress in understanding each other's feelings, they were dying to meet him. Emma was curious, too, about the people in California.

Last night he'd driven up I-5 to Seattle for a seminar today at The Four Seasons. He'd invited her to go along, but she had already promised to help out at a baby shower for one of her new friends from work.

Morgan had called her this morning before she left and again during his lunch break. He was coming straight here from his three-hour drive back. She wondered if he had given thought to the fact that, as of tonight, they had officially been seeing each other for two weeks.

After she finished applying a smudge of blue-gray shadow to her eyelids, she curled and darkened her lashes. The citrus scent she misted along her throat, Morgan's particular favorite, matched the lotion she had smoothed over the rest of her body after her shower.

Humming along with the Randy Travis classic on the radio, she fiddled with her hair. For once the waves that kept it from being either curly and cute or smooth and silky didn't give her grief.

"Good hair day," she crowed to Posy, who was too busy washing her paws to look up.

Sliding her hands lightly down her silk-clad hips, Emma danced over to the box that held her few pieces of decent jewelry. She had just poked one black pearl stud through the hole in her earlobe when her phone rang.

"Hello?"

"Miss me?" Morgan asked. As always, his deep voice stirred her senses like a wooden spoon cutting through a bowl of peanut butter fudge.

Cradling the receiver against her shoulder, she put on her other earring.

"Are you on your way home?" She didn't bother to hide her excitement.

"I'm afraid not, honey."

As she realized that no traffic noises sounded in the background, she swallowed her disappointment. Even though he had sworn that nothing short of an earthquake would delay his departure from Seattle when the seminar was done, she wasn't about to remind him. She didn't want to come across as a nag.

"Where are you, then?" she asked. "Stuck in Emerald City?"

"Wrong again."

His tone fueled her disappointment, pulling her lip into a pout. He didn't have to sound so damn cheerful about it!

"Right now I'm standing in front of your apartment," he added. "How about letting me in?"

With a whoop of excitement, Emma dropped the phone onto the bed and bolted for the front door. When she got there, she skidded to a stop, tugged on the neckline of her dress to make sure everything was in its proper place and took a deep breath.

When she yanked open the door, Morgan swooped down before she could say a word. Pulling her into his arms, he plundered her mouth in a kiss that was hot enough to crack the polish on her freshly painted toenails.

Emma clamped her hands on the sides of his head as she returned the kiss. At the same time, she wrapped one leg around his and plastered herself as close to his body as she could.

"Wait, wait," he groaned as he finally broke for air. "Let me get inside before we end up in separate cells down at the local jailhouse."

"On what charges?" she murmured against his throat as she allowed him to back her through the door. "We're consenting adults."

"Arson," he gasped, "for burning this place to the ground."

Together they got inside. After Morgan kicked the door shut behind him, he scooped her into his arms.

"Nice dress," he observed, looking at her cleavage. "I like what's not there the best."

"Animal." She swatted his shoulder.

"I missed you, honey." He spun her around in a dizzy circle before collapsing onto the couch with her more or less across his lap.

Clinging like a burr, she strung kisses down his jaw to his mouth. Beneath her hip, she could feel the gratifying strength of his response.

"I missed you, too," she told him as she straightened up, straddling him with her dress hiked up her thighs. She smiled into his eyes. "How many days have you been gone? Three? Four?"

"A month, at least," he muttered as he tipped his face toward hers. After another long kiss, he skimmed his hands up her legs to lift her off his lap and set her down next to him.

"Where's Posy?" he asked, glancing around. The two of them had bonded, pleasing Emma.

"On the bed," she replied. "How was the seminar?"

He shrugged. "Typical. The baby brunch?"

She arched her brows. "Typical," they both said in unison.

"This is getting a little scary," Emma said when they were done laughing like a couple of kids on a sugar high.

Morgan's expression sobered. "I brought you something."

"Cool," she exclaimed. "I love presents." She didn't

see a package, so she gave him an exaggerated leer. "Want me to search your pockets?"

Ignoring her joke, he just looked at her. "First I have something to ask you," he said, pressing her hand between both of his.

All the breath left her lungs in a silent whoosh, but then she realized that he wasn't the type of man who would be impulsive enough to pop some traditional question anywhere near this soon. Maybe he was going to ask if she wanted to move in with him, but even that would be a leap for a methodical man like Morgan.

Not that he was a plodder, not exactly. Just organized and cautious.

"What is it?" she asked with a smile of encouragement.

"Do you want me to show you the file on your birth parents?"

Emma's mouth dropped open and she gaped at him as her mind worked over the meaning behind what he'd just asked.

"Emma?" he asked when she continued to stare. "Honey?"

"What? What did you just ask me?" she demanded, feeling dizzy from the shock. Was this some cruel joke? Payback for her stupid seduction plan?

"I'm dead serious here," he continued. "I'll show you the file. You deserve to see it."

"Really?" Her voice almost squeaked. "You asked? You got permission?"

His gaze slid away from hers. "Not exactly."

The truth hit her like a wet washcloth to the side of her face.

"Oh my God!" she exclaimed as happiness flooded her system and tears of joy filled her eyes. "You love me!" She threw her arms around his neck, burying her face into his shoulder. "You love me!" she repeated with growing wonder, this time in a whisper.

He patted her back as though he were burping a baby. "Yes, I do," he murmured with a dry chuckle. "What tipped you off?"

She let go of her stranglehold on his neck so she could beam up at him through her tears. "You offered to compromise your principles for me."

He frowned and harrumphed. "Well, uh, I suppose. I've thought about it a lot and it means so much to you." He slipped his arm around her. "It would have to be our secret, though. I hope you understand."

For a moment she took a slow breath, letting herself feel the excitement of being so close to the truth. Then she grabbed a tissue from the box on the end table, wiping her tears. She knew what she had to do.

"It will have to remain *your* secret," she corrected him firmly. "But I appreciate your offer more than I can say."

"Excuse me?" Morgan's entire spine appeared to have stiffened as he searched her face.

"I can't let you do it," she said. "The guilt would give you an ulcer."

"No. No, really. The offer was a genuine one. I meant what I said."

She shook her head. "Uh-uh."

"Are you sure?" he asked slowly. "If you change your mind later..."

She patted his hand. "Oh, I'm not giving up. If I'm meant to find them, I will." She sighed, dismissing the burning ache of regret in her chest. "But I'll have to do it without compromising your principles."

Driven by her selfish quest, she had already disappointed him once and very badly. She was fortunate that he had given her a handful of second chances—the position at camp, the job at Children's Connection, and now all this. Nothing would ever make her hurt him again, not if she could help it.

"I swear to you that my offer wasn't some kind of sick test, Emma. I just never expected you to refuse."

"Thank you," she repeated. "Now where's my present?"

He didn't answer. "You love me, too," he said instead.

"Yes, I do love you," she confessed.

He fumbled into the pocket of his slacks. "I know it hasn't been very long," he said, clearing his throat nervously.

Emma's eyes nearly fell out of her head when she saw the small velvet box in his hand. *Calm yourself,* she ordered silently. It was probably a birthstone ring.

While she continued to stare, he slid off the couch

onto his knee and took her hand. His hand, she noticed through the pink mist of joy that threatened to envelop her brain, was trembling.

"People who know me will probably tell you that I haven't done anything impulsive since I was ten and I traded my Smith Miller log truck for a giant chocolate bar." His blue eyes seemed to burn with intensity. "They're probably right. When you meet the one special woman you've been searching for, you just know. It's time to take that leap."

She opened her mouth and closed it a couple of times without emitting any sound. Realizing she must look like a fish, she pressed her lips together.

"How can you be so sure?" she breathed. Same reason she was sure, she realized. It came from the heart, not the head.

He tapped his chest with the fingers of his free hand, as though he'd read her mind. "It spoke. I listened."

"Oh, my," she murmured. "My mom is just going to adore you."

Suddenly her smile wavered. "You'll want a family." Regret, bitter and vile, poured over her, pulled her back from him. "You know I have problems in that particular area."

"I want that family with you." He crushed her fingers in his. "I'll tell you right now that whatever way works for you, works for me. Mother Nature, in vitro, some other procedure, adoption, an alien baby we find under a cabbage leaf." He shrugged. "It makes no difference to me as long as you're the mom and I'm the dad."

"I love you, Morgan," she choked. This man, she knew, wouldn't walk away if the going got rough. He'd stick.

"I love you, too." One-handed, he popped the ring box open to reveal a flash of fire, an oval-cut diamond set between two smaller stones on a gold band. "If you don't like this—"

Before he could finish, she pressed her fingers to his lips, shushing him.

"That's the first dumb thing you've said since you got here."

"Is that a yes?" he asked.

A surge of happiness threatened to keep her from speaking, so she bobbed her head energetically and stuck out her hand.

"Yes," she finally managed to whisper as Morgan slid the beautiful ring onto her finger. Cupping her face in his big tanned hands, he followed it up with a kiss.

* * * * *

*Turn the page for a sneak preview
of the next emotional* LOGAN'S LEGACY *title,
ROYAL AFFAIR
by bestselling author Laurie Paige
on sale in August 2004...*

One

Ivy Crosby stood in the checkout line at the drugstore and wished someone would remove the display of gilt-framed mirrors, marked down fifty percent for quick sale, from the wall to her right. The mirrors reflected multiple images and she really didn't want to see herself just now.

With a grimace she reached up to tuck a strand of hair behind her ear. It didn't stay, of course.

Her hair was naturally blond, not always an asset, and naturally curly, which meant it did as it pleased. On an impulse she couldn't explain, she'd had the long tresses cut off last week.

A mistake, that. Now it lay in ringlets around her

face, making her look about seven instead of twenty-seven. She was also cursed with big blue eyes and a natural fringe of dark lashes that curled at the tips just like her hair.

The combination lent her a fragile innocence that was sometimes useful in business, but was mostly irritating, as people took her at face value.

Because of her looks, she'd been treated like a pet or a doll all her life. By family. By teachers. By boyfriends who'd been protective and possessive, as if they wanted to put her in a pocket and only let her out when it was convenient. For them.

Except for one man. Once upon a fairy-tale time out of time, she'd met her prince—a man who'd treated her as a woman, a very desirable woman, an equal in wit, intelligence…and passion.

Oh, yes, passion. A faint tremor ran through her blood, the first warning of the volcanic explosion that was to come. Just the thought of him, six weeks later, could do that to her.

Max. I need you.

No, she mentally chided. She was an adult and she could figure this out. But first things first, as one of her business professors used to say. That's why she was at this pharmacy in a strip mall where she wasn't likely to be recognized.

Her many images glowered at her from the mirrors. She smoothed out the frown and laid her purchases on the counter. She'd gotten lotion and shampoo and a couple of other things she didn't need in hopes that no one would notice she'd also gotten a pregnancy test kit.

"Sorry, I have to change the tape," the clerk said, opening the top of the cash register and removing the spent roll of paper. When she attempted to thread the new roll through the machine, it jammed. The woman muttered a curse.

Ivy tamped down the impatience that made her want to turn and walk out as fast as she could. She'd stood in line this long, what was a few more minutes? Besides, she would have to do it all over again someplace else.

Schooling herself to calmness, she absently glanced over the tabloids while she waited. The headlines were amusing as usual, Woman Gives Birth to Martian and other interesting tidbits.

She skimmed the large print. A movie star was getting a divorce. Ho-hum. The Lion Roars, proclaimed another above a picture of a handsome man holding the arm of a fragile beauty—

Ivy gasped. She grabbed the edge of the counter as the room went into a dangerous spin.

"Are you all right?" the clerk asked, leaning close and peering into her eyes.

Ivy blinked several times and the world righted itself. Except for the abyss giving way under her feet. "Yes, just a…a sort of…of a dizzy spell. I'm fine now." She smiled to prove that she was.

The clerk nodded sympathetically. "When I was pregnant with my first, I fainted at the drop of a hat. Blood was especially bad. My sister cut her finger one night when we were having dinner at her place. I fell right out on the kitchen floor. Scared my husband to death. He didn't know I was expecting. Neither did I, come to think of it."

Ivy dredged up a smile while the clerk and the woman behind her in line laughed nostalgically. "I'll take this, too," she said, and put the tabloid on the counter.

By the time she'd paid cash for her purchases and rushed to her car, every nerve in her body was quivering like an aspen leaf in a playful breeze. She tossed her purchases into the passenger seat, grabbed the tabloid and read the article that went with the headline.

Her eyes widened and narrowed by turns as she skimmed through the hyperbole to get to the meat of the story. It seemed Prince Maxwell von Husden, Crown Prince of Lantanya, who was soon to be king, had been seen at a popular tourist resort in the tiny country with a mysterious beauty in July. After a romantic night of dining and dancing and passion, the woman had disappeared.

Ivy gasped and felt faint again. How could they have known about the passion?

Reporters always made up the stuff to fill in the

blanks, she decided grimly, trying to calm the emotions that roared through her like a tsunami. She read on.

The prince was furious that the woman had slipped out on him before he grew bored and dropped her, according to one "close palace source." Another source contended that the prince was heartbroken but covering it with anger.

Ivy pressed a hand to her thundering heart. "Liar," she said. She'd been right to leave without waking him the next morning, although it had been difficult to do.

He'd looked so handsome lying in the king-size bed, his hair mussed and a morning beard shadowing his face, his expression one of contentment. She'd contemplated kissing him goodbye, but she'd had a plane to catch and she wasn't sure they could stop at one kiss.

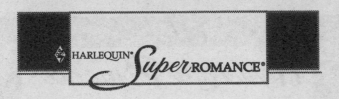

HARLEQUIN®
INTRIGUE

WE'LL LEAVE YOU BREATHLESS!

If you've been looking for thrilling tales of
contemporary passion and sensuous love stories
with taut, edge-of-the-seat suspense—then
you'll love Harlequin Intrigue!

Every month, you'll meet four new heroes
who are guaranteed to make your spine tingle
and your pulse pound. With them you'll enter
into the exciting world of Harlequin Intrigue—
where your life is on the line
and so is your heart!

THAT'S INTRIGUE—
ROMANTIC SUSPENSE
AT ITS BEST!

HARLEQUIN®
Makes any time special ®

Visit us at www.eHarlequin.com

INTDIR1